To Maria Aquino,
who brought her own special
magic into our lives,

and

to Gloria Catanzaro,
for never making excuses for the
behavior of her husband, Michael.

The Misfit Apprentice

The Misfit
Apprentice

Robert Levy

Houghton Mifflin Company
Boston 1995

Library of Congress Cataloging-in-Publication Data

Levy, Robert, 1945–
    The misfit apprentice / by Robert Levy.
        p.   cm.
    Summary: Fifteen-year-old Maria, a failed apprentice magician who
has trouble controlling her magic, joins the mute boy, Tristan, in
entering the country of their enemies to search for the lost magic
scrolls.
    ISBN 0-395-68077-8
    [1. Fantasy.]   I. Title.
PZ7.L5836Lo   1995   93-1575
[Fic] — dc20   CIP
                              AC

Printed in the United States of America
HAD 10   9   8   7   6   5   4   3   2   1

The Misfit
Apprentice

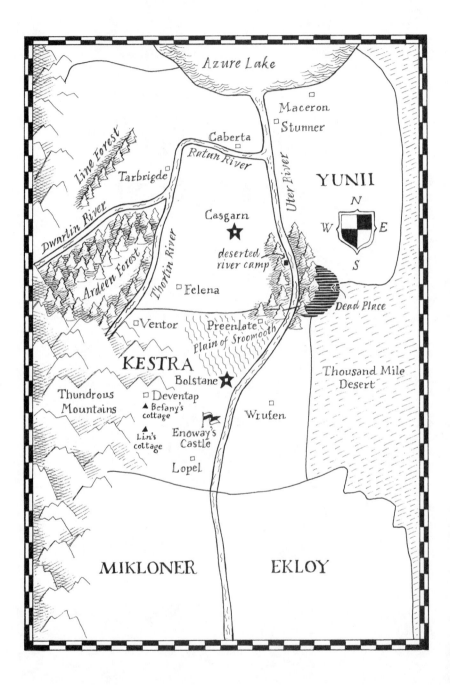

Chapter 1

From her hidden perch high on the mountain ledge, Maria watched Queen Andraya's army moving slowly through the narrow ravine cut deeply below. *I begged the queen not to go this way,* thought Maria. *I told her it was a perfect place for an ambush.*

But the queen wouldn't listen to a fifteen-year-old, no matter how powerful a magician she was. Now the whole army was vulnerable. Just then, Maria heard them: war horns blown by men concealed on the steep slopes. Shouts of "Long live the king! Long live Yunii!" echoed off the mountainsides. Buckets of burning oil, hurled upward by camouflaged catapults, arched into the sky and began their long fall. As soon as the first volley was in the air, men who had been hiding behind rocks stood and rained arrows toward the trapped army. They screamed King Helborat's name as they fired arrow after arrow. By now, the first fire buckets had crashed into the queen's soldiers, and their cries mingled with the calls of victory from Helborat's soldiers. In a matter of minutes, Queen Andraya would be dead . . . unless . . .

Maria left her hiding place and walked to the end of the

ledge. The wind howled; it blew her hood onto her shoulders, whipped the long blue robe straight back, and tried to push her away. But Maria wouldn't budge. She raised her arms as if to hug the horizon and called: "Earth, air, fire, water, come to me, strengthen me." Her shoulders shuddered; her breath quickened. The forces of magic surrounded her and waited until she muttered the words of an ancient spell. Maria spoke — lightning flashed, each bolt aimed at places where Helborat's men hid. Water poured out of holes that suddenly opened in the white clouds and drenched the fires. Her arms still up, Maria saw huge boulders sliding down. Her eyes narrowed; she bit her bottom lip. If the landslides went unchecked, they would do Helborat's work for him and bury the queen. *That cannot happen!*

While the still-spearing lightning destroyed Andraya's enemy, Maria called out another spell. The earth loosened its grip and falling boulders as large as horses became feather-light, floating softly down; Andraya's soldiers had no trouble avoiding them. What had started as the end of Queen Andraya's reign now ended in the certainty that she would rule Kestra for many years to come.

Maria lowered her arms. The magic left. All was silent. She stared down and saw the faces below watching her. Shouts floated on the wind and hung in the air like a crown around her head. Chills raced along her back and neck. "Maria! Maria! Maria!"

Maria smiled. No one would ever doubt her again. No one would ever call her inept again. The next time she spoke to Andraya, the queen would listen. Maria had not only saved the kingdom but had proved to everyone that she was more than just a Magician of the First Order. She was a true sorceress.

"Maria! Maria! Are you in there?" Maria shook her head. Images of an entire army chanting her name vanished as suddenly as her dream had created them. Again she heard someone call. Closing the book she was supposed to be reading, she got up to open the door. Reena, the serving girl who worked in the magician's tower, stood there. "Mistress Eonoway wants you!" Without bowing, Reena turned and left.

What did I do now? Maria thought as she put her spell book in her pocket and ran down the long flight of sharply curving steps. She jumped the last four steps, slamming heavily on the stone floor. She stopped. *Don't run! Eonoway told me too many times.* Taking a deep breath, she walked calmly the rest of the way to Eonoway's study. The wooden door opened silently as she raised her hand to knock. Eonoway was sitting behind the large desk, face buried in papers. "Come in."

"Yes, Mistress," answered Maria, bowing from the waist. The door closed with a bang, and the echo took several seconds to pass. The sound startled Maria — she flinched. Eonoway shook her head. *Something's wrong,* thought Maria. *The chair I always sit in when I have my lessons is in the corner.* Maria stood in front of the desk waiting for Eonoway to say something. But the magician didn't speak. Instead, she stared at Maria with large brown eyes, occasionally glancing at the paper she held.

Maria was nervous. Her breakfast began to inch its way toward her throat. She swallowed hard, hoping Eonoway would not think the noise impolite. Quickly, Maria went over the assignments Eonoway had given her during the past week. She had finished them all, though half of them didn't come out the way they were supposed to. But she hadn't messed up, at least not in any major way. She hadn't started a fire where it wasn't wanted, made a hole in the tower wall, or caused the well to overflow and flood the kitchen floor. She had done all of those when she was a beginning apprentice. She was better now. Or was she?

"Maria," said Eonoway, breaking the silence with a soft feathery voice, "how old are you?"

"Fifteen, Mistress."

"How long have you apprenticed with me?"

"Three years, Mistress."

"Do you think you have learned enough to become a lesser magician?"

"No, Mistress."

"How long does it take an average apprentice to wear the brown robe of a lesser magician?"

This time, Maria didn't answer. She lowered her head and stared at her feet. Her breakfast swirled in her stomach. All the feelings of failure that she had tried to hide during the last year poured into her. All the whispered voices of the servants calling her "incompetent" and "unworthy" returned to her ears. She closed her eyes tightly and recited a calming spell to stop the tears from escaping.

"When you came here," said Eonoway, pretending not to notice the struggle going on inside Maria, "I thought you would be my finest pupil. Of the ninety-seven girls who wanted to apprentice with me, you had the most innate power. You have more native ability than anyone I have ever taught. I had hopes for you, Maria, hopes that one day you would become a Magician of the First Order, not just a lesser magician like all my other pupils. I even thought that you might sit next to me on the Council. But . . ." Eonoway hesitated as she straightened the papers on her desk, "I don't know what more I can do. Maybe your lack of progress is my fault."

Maria looked up, no longer trying to hold back the tears. "It's not your fault, Mistress. You have showed me every kindness. You have been the most patient teacher anyone could have wanted. I guess being a magician is harder than I thought."

"Nonsense!" said Eonoway, raising her voice for the first time. "It is not a matter of difficulty. It is a matter of listening, learning, and performing the spells the way they are supposed to be done, not by performing them the way you think they should be done. It is a matter of concentrating on your work, no matter how dull or insignificant you think that work may be. How many times have I told you to keep your mind focused on being a magician even when sitting in a tub? How many times have I told you that magicians never run downstairs because it breaks their concentration? How many times have I told you that being a magician must occupy your mind twenty-four hours a day, not just for a few moments before you practice your spells? And how many times have I told you that day-dreaming only hinders your learning? It steals your mind away from reality and lets you wander in dreams where everyone, even the lowliest peasant, is a mighty hero! You do not need imagination to be a magician, Maria. You need discipline."

"I'm sorry, Mistress. I will try harder. I promise I will."

Eonoway let out a deep breath. "When you first came here, I told you magic was not an exact science. Even I, a Magician of the First Order, can accomplish a task one day, but find it impossible to do the next. Magic is very strange, Maria. It follows a law of its own, a law we don't understand. But I succeed more of the time than not, and that's what makes me what I am. That, child, is what discipline does, and that is exactly what you lack." She picked up the letter from the top of the pile she had made, looked at it for a moment, then opened her hand to let the paper float back.

"Maria, I like you and wish things could be different. But things cannot always be as one likes. Queen Andraya has summoned the full Council to her."

"But why? What is the matter?"

"King Helborat. You know he has been preparing his army for war. He dreams of becoming an emperor. We thought he would wait until next spring, but our spies in Yunii have sent word to the queen that Helborat's army will attack Kestra before summer. Tomorrow I travel to Bolstane. I don't know when I'll return. I'm sorry, Maria, but you must leave today."

Leave! "But . . . but what will I do? Where will I go?"

"All of your belongings, all of the things that you will be allowed to take, are packed and waiting outside in the courtyard." Eonoway leaned over and dropped a small pouch that jingled when it touched the desktop. "There is enough money in there to last half a year, if you're careful. That's time enough to find another profession."

"But I don't want another profession. You know my parents are dead and I have nowhere to go. I want . . ." Maria stopped. When she looked into Eonoway's eyes, she knew there was nothing she could say that would make the magician change her mind. She reached out with a shaking hand and took the pouch. "Thank you," she whispered.

"I will need your spell book."

My spell book! "But . . ."

"Remember the vow you took when you first came. All that you learn, all that you do, must never be told to anyone outside the Order of Magicians. Though you're no longer an apprentice, that vow still binds you." Eonoway rose, placing both her hands on the desk. She spoke very slowly now. "If you ever break it, if you ever tell anyone about your lessons within these walls, your life is forfeit. Do you understand?"

"Yes, Mistress."

"Your spell book."

Slowly, Maria put her spell book on the desk and headed for the door. Eonoway's voice stopped her.

"There is power in you, child. A power that not even I was able to bring forth. I'm sorry. But listen well, now. The first day you came I told you that to be a true magician, you must believe in yourself. I know you had trouble learning your lessons and will probably soon forget what little you've learned. But remember always that first lesson. *Believe in yourself.*"

"I will try, Mistress," said Maria, wiping her eyes with the sleeve of her shirt.

"I will hold you to that promise, Maria. You are dismissed."

"Yes, Mistress. And thank you." For the last time, Maria Ronlin bowed to Eonoway, Magician of the First Order, then turned and walked through the door that opened before her and shut silently behind.

Chapter 2

Though it was nearly midday and the courtyard should have been busy with people, it was empty except for a small donkey laden with two packs. Maria walked to it and petted its nose.

"Hello, Tiny," she whispered. "At least Eonoway let me take you." Tiny pushed his face against her chest and snorted. Maria started walking. She felt eyes staring at her, the eyes of servants hiding behind the half-opened doors and windows. She wanted to call out, telling them they were wrong and that one day she *would* be a magician. But she didn't. She just stared at her feet as she crossed the lowered drawbridge. The rusty chains creaked as the drawbridge rose behind her. Maria trudged down the dusty road holding Tiny's reins so tightly that her hand began to hurt. When the path curved and the castle disappeared from view, she stopped and looked behind at the empty road. Her eyes teared and she wiped them with her fingers. She didn't want to cry but couldn't help it.

For the past three years, even though she was never a good apprentice, she had been happy. *Learning magic takes time. Eonoway herself said that. I can't help it if I need more time than others. Now I'll never be a magician. I have enough money to last for several months, but what then? I have to find another trade. Who's going to train me? Apprentices start when they're twelve. Who would want me now? Besides, I don't want to do anything else. I want to be a magician!* Her arm jerked when Tiny started to graze on the grass growing along the side of the road.

"Come on, Tiny," she said, rubbing her eyes. "Let's go. We'll figure out what to do tomorrow."

Tomorrow came and went. So did several others, and still Maria hadn't decided. A week later, a dirty, tired, former magician's apprentice camped near a stream. The water was still icy with the runoff from the last winter's snow but Maria didn't mind. She sat in the center of the stream and scrubbed herself clean, using the sand from the bottom. Afterward, she washed her clothes. Then she sat by a fire to keep away the chill of the early spring night. The dress she now wore was too thin for the time of year, but until the other one dried, it was all she had.

Since Maria had left the castle, she was always hungry. Eonoway had given her several weeks' worth of journey cakes and dried meat strips, but Maria had no idea how long they would have to last. Until she decided where to go, she avoided the small villages dotting the main road to Bolstane. So far, doing that had been easy. All the villages were at least a mile from the main road because the ground in this part of Kestra was so rocky that the earth couldn't be plowed. The road wound its way through patches of forested land and bare ground where nothing grew but

10

rocks. Only when the road neared Bolstane did the villages spring up next to it.

Bolstane. I wish I could have gone there. Maria had often dreamed of that. But in her dreams, she rode a magnificent warhorse and wore the purple cape of a full magician. Now she would have been content to enter at the end of Eonoway's party wearing only the faded brown of a lesser magician. *No, I can't go to Bolstane. People who have their pick of apprentices will ask me what have I been doing for the past three years. They'll laugh when I tell them. But where will I go?*

Maria looked up and thought about the future as the twin moons appeared over the treetops. It was hard to see Bern because its smaller brother, Pern, was directly in front of it. Maria watched them for a moment, and then saw Bern's edge peek through. Pern constantly revolved around Bern, and little eclipses like this happened very often. Tiny interrupted her thinking when he walked closer to the fire. His head was up; his ears were twitching.

Maria threw several branches on the fire and moved nervously closer to it. The flames leaped higher. A twig snapped — her heart beat faster. She closed her eyes and concentrated on a calming exercise. She relaxed and took the magician's pose, arms crossed diagonally over her chest, palms open, resting just below her shoulders. It was impossible to remember all the spells Eonoway had tried to teach her. That's why Maria had written them down in her spell book. Now, without that book . . . again, a noise reached out from the darkness. Someone was hiding in the

11

trees just beyond the edge of the fire's light, and Maria could do nothing. *I have to remember my spells!*

Maria listened; she heard Tiny nearby, eating grass. "You think whoever was there went away?" she whispered to her donkey. Tiny twitched his ears and continued to eat. Maria recited a spell that would heighten her senses if it worked, but it didn't. The darkness was still black; the only thing she heard was the wood popping in the fire.

Maria let out a deep sigh, stood up, and faced the direction she thought the sound had come from. "Who's there?" Silence was all that answered. "Who's there?" she called again. Sweat beaded on her palms, and she rubbed them together before reluctantly taking the magician's stance again. *This one will work. It's an easy one.*

Slowly, Maria chanted a seeking spell. To get it to work, the spell had to be recited three times. Though the words were the same, each time different syllables had to be accented. Maria had often asked why that was necessary, but the only answer she had ever received was a scornful look from her teacher. "Do it the way you were told," Eonoway had said.

> "Me HA-da keynote eesTAR bremTO.
> ME ha-da KEYnote EEStar BREMto.
> Me ha-DA keyNOTE EESTAR bremto."

A bubble of light grew around her. Slowly it floated up and off to her left, disappearing into the trees. Just beyond the edge of the fire, the bubble descended on someone sitting on a branch. Maria forgot to breathe as a young man in the light turned his head and stared at her. He jumped down and ran into the darkness. "Stop!" shouted Maria. But he had vanished.

Maria lowered her arms; the magic light disappeared. *Who was he?* she wondered as she sat. *I think he was my age. What did he want? His clothes were almost rags and he was as dirty as I was before I bathed. Did he want to steal from me? No. If he did, he would have just taken Tiny while I was in the water. While I was . . . was he here then? Did he see me!* Maria inched closer to the fire, holding her blanket tighter. After finishing a journey cake, she thought about the young man again. *He didn't try to hurt me, and he was so thin. Maybe he was . . .*

Maria took out several cakes and meat strips and, holding a branch from the fire as a torch, walked to the tree the young man had been sitting in. "This is for you," she called into the night. She left the food on the branch and returned to her fire. Sitting still and remembering, she crossed her arms and whispered a sealing spell, one designed to protect a magician. This spell, like most others, had no bubble of light to tell her if it worked or not. She put her head down on her pack and slept, never knowing whether the spell or merely luck had kept her safe during the night.

She was awakened in the morning by the sun's first rays. Tiny had wandered toward the stream, making a breakfast of the early spring grass. Maria's first thought was for the stranger she had seen the night before. She wrapped the blanket around her as she went to the tree. The food was gone. *I hope he ate it instead of some hungry animal.* Her

13

woolen dress was not dry, so after getting Tiny ready, she draped it over her packs. She kept the blanket out to use as a shawl.

A few minutes' walk through the trees brought her to a crossroad. There was a post with the names of Kestra's four largest cities written on wooden arrows pointing in four different directions. Bolstane was north, straight ahead. Lopel was behind her; since that was the way she had come, she wouldn't go there. The road to the right led to Wruten, and the last road, heading west, ended in Deventap, near the Thundrous Mountains.

"That's where we'll go, Tiny. Deventap. It's not big enough to draw lots of people so we might find work. Who knows, maybe no one will ask me what I've been doing these past three years. It's possible they'll just be happy to have someone working for them." Maria wasn't very enthusiastic about going there but Tiny didn't seem to mind. He waited for her to stop talking and start walking.

Later that day, the road twisted sharply to the right. Maria and Tiny turned the corner and stopped. Facing them was a small wooden bridge no more than twenty feet long. Blocking the bridge was a pole resting in the notches of two boulders, one on each side of the road. Four men sat on the ground in front of it, playing a dice game. They were so involved that none of them noticed Maria and Tiny. She peeked over the edge of the road to see if there was another way to cross. Below the bridge ran a long, narrow crevasse, a crack in the earth left over from some forgotten earthquake. If she wanted to go to Deventap, she'd have to cross the bridge.

The two walked toward the men. When they saw the girl with her donkey, one man got up.

"Toll's three coppers."

"What toll?"

"Toll to cross the bridge. Who do you think pays for its upkeep?" Two of the men laughed.

Maria looked beyond the man to the bridge. It was obviously in need of repair — there were splits in the plank floor and the railing was completely missing on one side. "I don't know. But this bridge hasn't been repaired in a long time."

"That's because there aren't many people going to Deventap these days. You want to cross? Toll's four coppers."

"I thought you said it was three?"

"What's one copper, more or less? You want to cross or not? I've got other things to do besides talking to children."

Maria's heart raced. She reached her hand into one of the packs tied to Tiny's saddle and thought. *These men are thieves. After three years of apprenticing, I should be able to stop them. If Eonoway were here she would cast a spell forcing the men to go to the nearest soldiers' garrison and confess their crime. I should be able to do something!* Her hand shivered inside the pack as she searched for the money pouch. *I can't remember the spells! And even if I could, they probably wouldn't work.* Then she felt the bag, loosened it, and slipped three coins into her palm. "Here. It's all I have."

"I told you the toll was four coppers," said the man, looking at the coins in his hand.

"And I told you it's all I have."

"Now that's strange," said another man. "A young girl like you traveling all alone with a well-fed donkey and two packs. Are you sure? Maybe we should look." The man dropped the dice and got up. The other two rose with him. "Let's see what you have in those packs, girl. Then we'll tell you the real toll."

A lump appeared in Maria's throat and she swallowed. As the men approached, her arms flew across her chest.

"KeeTOEme breURAL VENA-ope.
KEEtoeME BREural vena-OPE."

The four men stopped and stared at each other. Then, all at the same time, they started to laugh. One of them laughed so hard he had to kneel down and put his hands on the ground.

Suddenly the man closest to Maria screamed. His hand went to his forehead and blood dripped through his open fingers. He took one step toward Maria, then his head flew back, his knees wavered, and he fell.

A second man rushed her. He, too, screamed. Blood poured out of a gash in the side of his head. He staggered backward against the pole, falling with it into the crevasse. The other two men ran.

Maria froze, holding on to Tiny's reins. *I pronounced the words correctly, I'm sure I did! They should have fallen asleep. What did I do? I don't know a spell that causes that to happen. COULD I have said the words wrong? IS there a spell that hurts people like that?*

A branch snapped from behind and Maria turned. Coming out of the bushes along the side of the road was

16

the same young man who had spied on her the night before, but now he held a sling hanging loosely in one hand.
He walked to the man on the ground without once looking at Maria, then stooped down and pried the man's
fingers open. Next, he walked to Maria, giving her three
copper coins. He pushed the sling into his belt and took
Tiny's reins. Motioning her to follow, he started across the
bridge. Before he stepped on the first plank, however, he
stopped, searched the ground, and picked up three small
round stones. Putting the stones back in his pocket, he
began again.

Maria, still rooted to the ground, swallowed. *I didn't do
anything. He hit the men with his rocks. Some magician I
am. I couldn't even cast a simple sleeping spell.* She recited
her calming spell, then followed Tiny and the young man
who had saved her.

"Thanks," said Maria when she caught up to him. He
turned and looked at her. He was still as dirty as he had
been before, with streaks of dried mud crisscrossing his
face. His shirt and pants were torn in several places and
both were too small. He stared at Maria with large black
eyes and, after a moment, handed her the reins and continued.

"Wait a minute!" Maria called after him. "Who are you?
Where did you come from?"

The young man stopped, turned to face Maria, and
shrugged his shoulders. Then he started walking.

Maria shook her head, not knowing what to do. But
Tiny knew. The donkey followed him. As she walked next
to Tiny, Maria thought, *He's not going to hurt me . . . he's
heading toward Deventap . . . maybe I should stay with*

him for a while? She ran a few steps to catch up. The youth slowed his pace but didn't look at her.

They walked together, silently, for over an hour. Maria kept looking at him. *Why isn't he saying anything? He knows I can do magic. Is he ashamed to be seen with me knowing I couldn't cast the sleeping spell?* "My name's Maria," she finally said. But he still didn't look at her or speak; he just kept walking.

At the beginning of a small patch of yellow-leafed frost trees, the road forked. Maria turned to the right toward Deventap. But the young man turned left, taking a much smaller path.

"Wait. Aren't you going to Deventap?"

He stopped.

"You're not going there, are you?"

For the first time since they met, he reacted to something she had said. He shook his head.

"Why do you want to go that way?"

But the young man didn't answer.

Maria still wasn't sure of his age due to the dirt, but judging by his height, he could have been fifteen or sixteen. His black eyes stared at her and she felt that, somehow, they were more than eyes. They looked deep into her. Maria thought that he not only saw her face, but saw her as she really was. Her shoulders quivered. In the few seconds that passed, it seemed as if this person knew everything about her there was to know, including her utter failure as a magician.

Ever since she went to live with Eonoway, Maria had been taught to think carefully about what magic she wanted to do, concentrate on it, and cast the spell. In fact, magicians, she had been told, never did *anything* on impulse. But now she did. Faced with going off by herself or staying with the strange youth who had saved her, Maria quickly chose. "Can I come with you?"

His shoulders shrugged. It could have meant yes or no. Maria took it for yes and continued walking with him. Soon the dusty path disappeared into a long grassy field, and at the far end was the beginning of a forest. They entered the woods, walking along a narrow path that wound its way through the trees. An hour later, Maria saw a cottage in the middle of a small field surrounded by trees. Sitting in a chair in front of the house was a man. Maria saw him better when he stood up; he was tall, with a gray-white beard, white hair, and walked with a limp.

"Hello," he said to Maria. Then he stared at the young man. "Tristan! You look like a walking mud puddle!" The boy raised his hands but the man went right on talking. "You should be ashamed of yourself, allowing anyone to see you in that condition. Get out of here! Go wash in the stream and don't come back until I can see your skin! And throw away those clothes!"

Tristan shrugged his shoulders and disappeared into the woods behind the house. The old man laughed as he reached Maria and took Tiny's reins. "I can understand a person having a favorite chair, or horse, or even a favorite blanket. But favorite clothes? Clothes a beggar wouldn't take? I don't think I'll ever understand him."

The man led Tiny to the side of the cottage and began unstrapping his packs. "That's a good boy. You need a good rubdown, don't you? You'll get that in a little while. For now, eat as much grass as you want." There was a long rope attached to a ring on the side of the house and the old man tied Tiny to it. "Let him graze. Later, after we've had a chance to talk, take a rag from that box and give him that rubdown."

"Yes . . ."

"Linster Talburt Grestin Feslit," said the man, starting to laugh. "But most people call me Lin. And you?

"Maria Ronlin."

"Well, Maria, come inside. Are you hungry? I was about to have lunch."

Lunch was not elaborate, but for Maria it was a feast. Bread and cheese, cold meat, and a steaming cup of tea. As they finished eating, Tristan came in.

"Now that's the way you should look," said Lin.

What a difference! With the dirt removed, Tristan was strikingly handsome. First of all, his brownish hair was really light blond. He had high cheekbones, dimples that could now be seen in both cheeks, and smooth, unblemished skin. His new clothes fit him. Though they weren't *new* new, they were clean and without holes. "Thank you for helping me, Tristan."

Tristan looked at her, then sat silently next to Lin.

Maria swallowed her last piece of cheese before speaking. "Is he always like this?"

"Don't mind him," said Lin. "He doesn't like people. Something happened to him when he was a young child, something he hasn't gotten over. But he will, one day, won't you Tristan?"

Tristan looked at Lin with the same blankness Maria had seen before and continued eating.

20

"What happened?" asked Maria.

"I don't know. I found him, lying unconscious with bruises all over his body, about eight years ago. It took him several weeks to recover. He never told me what happened. As a matter of fact, he never told me anything. He hasn't made a sound in all the time we've lived together. But enough of him. Tell me about yourself. Who are you? Where are you coming from? Where are you going?"

Maria hesitated at first, not knowing what to say. But as Lin poured her another cup of tea and Tristan started to play a soft tune on a lute, Maria felt very comfortable. The music was soothing, and almost before she realized it, she had told Lin and Tristan everything about herself. When she finished, Lin just shook his head and smiled. Though Maria felt tears welling up in her eyes, she sipped her tea and smiled back.

"I want you to try something," said Lin. He left the cottage, returning a moment later carrying a piece of wood with a small circular hole cut from its center. Next, he pulled out a wooden doorstop. "Maria, I'd like you to take this wood and put it through the hole."

"The hole's too small," said Maria, picking up the doorstop. She tried several times, holding the wedge at different angles, but nothing she could do would force the wood through the opening. "It's impossible," she finally said.

Lin laughed. "Listen carefully, Maria. I will tell you a secret so simple that very few people ever discover it on their own. The difference between possible and impossible is often the limit of your imagination."

"I don't understand."

"Tristan," said Lin. "Can you put the wedge through the hole?"

Tristan put the lute down and got a small hand axe. He placed the wedge on the floor and, with one swing, split it in two. Each piece was now small enough to pass through the hole.

"That's not fair! You didn't tell me I could cut the wood."

"I didn't tell you you couldn't. I didn't give you any guidelines. All I told you was what I wanted done. The restraints you put on yourself were the limits of your own mind. If you had let your imagination run free you might have solved the problem."

"But magic's not the same. You have to do it the way they say. Eonoway told me that the first day I came to live with her."

"Magicians!" said Lin. "They force their apprentices to do everything the same way they do. It's like making everyone wear the same size shoes. But Maria, people don't all have the same size feet. If you want to be a magician, you have to understand that."

"But the spells. They have to be spoken in certain ways or else they don't work. Believe me, I know."

"You told me you pronounced that sleep spell correctly. Then why didn't it work?"

Now Maria's eyes did tear up. "I'm not good enough," she whispered.

Lin laughed as he shook his head. "Nonsense. If you didn't have talent, Eonoway would never have selected you in the first place. And if that Magician of the First Order had any imagination herself, you wouldn't be here now. Come to the window."

Maria got up and followed. She saw Tiny twitching his ears, rubbing himself against a small tree.

"Put Tiny to sleep," said Lin.

Maria took a deep breath and crossed her arms over her chest. Lin gently took Maria's wrists and pushed her arms down. "That's their way. The Order of Magician's way doesn't work for you. That means you have one of two choices. Either give up wanting to be a magician or find your own way of doing magic."

"How can you find your own way? Spells are spells. Eonoway says them and they work most of the time. I say them and they don't work any of the time. There can't be a second way to do magic. There's only one way. It's impossible to find your own way."

Lin shook his head. "You said that with the wood. Try it. You have nothing to lose. But try it your way, not Eonoway's. Close your eyes and say the magic the way that seems natural to you, the way you want to, not the way your teacher wanted."

Maria didn't know what to think as Lin backed up. Tristan had gone back to playing his lute and the room was bathed in its soft melody. Maria didn't need her calming spell. She felt relaxed and at ease. After staring at Tiny for a moment, she closed her eyes. She thought about the words and whispered them only once in regular speech.

"Keetoeme breural vena-ope."

When her eyes opened, Tiny was lying with his head on the grass. "I did it!"

"Yes, you did," said Lin softly. "Now go wake him up and give him that rubdown I promised. Tristan and I will unpack your bags. When you come back, we'll talk."

Chapter 3

Maria was still brushing Tiny when she heard horses galloping through the woods. She stopped and, walking to the front of the cottage, saw Tristan playing his lute. Lin was in his chair carving a figure from a tree branch. Within seconds, two dozen riders, the lead one carrying the purple banner of Queen Andraya, broke through the trees and approached.

The riders stopped and one took out a scroll. "Name?"

"Linster Talburt Grestin Feslit."

The man ran his fingers down the scroll, mouthing the names he passed until he came to Lin's name. "Twenty-one coppers or seven silvers."

"This isn't tax time," answered Lin.

"Helborat's army is moving south. Rumor has it his troops will be in striking distance of our border by the end of the week. Crazy of him, too. Our army's superior. We train our soldiers much better than they do in Yunii. It shouldn't take us long to win, maybe until late fall. That's why the special tax is so low."

"You sound as if we have won already," said Lin.

"You're very confident. Tell me, captain, have you ever seen a war?"

"Not yet, but it's time I did more with this sword than practice. Be careful, old man. Reports say raiding parties have slipped past our mountain garrisons and are in this area. That's why we ride in force. I'd move into Deventap until reinforcements arrive."

"Thank you, Captain. We'll think about it." Lin got up and went into the cottage. He returned a moment later with a small pouch that he threw in the air. The captain caught it and without counting, put it into his saddlebag. Lin shook his head when they left. "War's not a game, my young captain," he said to the air. "People die in wars, and if Andraya isn't careful, more people will die than she realizes. Her new son may never grow up to be a king, and you, my children, may grow up to be slaves."

"Why do you say that?" asked Maria.

"Queen Andraya will trust her magicians, and for the first time in their lives, they will come across a magic they cannot defend against. I told them that once, a long time ago. They didn't listen then, and it's too late now."

"I don't understand. What did you say to whom?"

"Come inside and I'll explain."

Once in the cottage, Lin and Maria took chairs next to the table while Tristan sat on the floor tuning his lute. "Magic, Maria, is inflexible. It is a force that exists around us, though I have no idea where it comes from. Maybe it appeared when Enstor was created and will continue to be here until our world no longer exists. Or maybe we'll wake up one morning and it will all be gone. For all we know, the fairy tales my parents told me about elves and dwarfs were true. Those faery folk were supposed to have brought the magic to Enstor when they appeared thousands of years ago. No one understands how magic got here or how it works. We just know it exists. Another thing no one can explain is why not everyone can perform magic or why those who can, can do it only some of the time. Maybe one person out of a thousand can say the spells and make the magic perform. Maybe it's only one out of every five thousand. But I don't have to tell you how hard it is to do magic."

Maria didn't answer. She just looked at Lin and shrugged her shoulders.

"You also know the Order of Magicians believes that to do magic properly, you must always say the spells in the same way. Any variation, according to them, produces either different effects or no effects."

"I know about that," said Maria. "I once made a hole in the tower wall."

"But it wasn't your fault. It was Eonoway's. She refused to accept the idea that your feet are different from hers." Maria squinted, and Lin paused a few seconds before continuing. "You have the ability to work magic, but for some reason, you can't do it most of the time. Therefore, you have to alter the way you speak to the magic in order to mold it to your inner self."

Maria let out a deep breath and shook her head.

"Let me try it another way. You remember when I asked you to put the wooden wedge through this?" He picked up the wood with the hole and dropped it on the table. "No matter what you did to the wedge, you couldn't put it through the hole. Imagine that magic is like this block of wood. In order to get it to perform, you say the spell, your words go through the hole, and the magic does what you want. But for some reason, when you say the magic the way Eonoway wants you to, your words won't fit through the hole. I told you that magic is inflexible. There's nothing you can do that will change the size of the magic hole. Just as Tristan split the wedge to make it fit, you have to change the way you recite the spells in order to get your words to fit. You have to do something to get the magic to obey you, something your teacher told you not to do. You have to use your imagination."

"Do you think that's why Tiny went to sleep?"

"Do you?"

That can't be true. If it is, then everything Eonoway taught me was wrong. "How do you know?" she said quietly.

Lin leaned back in the chair before answering. "Once, a long time ago, I was elected to the First Order of Magicians."

The First Order! Maria sat up straighter in her chair.

"I realized after I began having my own students that not everyone who had talent could perform magic. They had the same problem you have. I wondered why and began researching it. That's when I discovered that all of the magic we know comes from a few ancient scrolls. No one knows who wrote them, or what language they were written in. We just know that when we pronounce certain phrases that were taken from those scrolls, the magic performs. The Order of Magicians' library has only twelve of the ancient scrolls. Most of Kestra's scrolls vanished ages ago. But I learned that a large collection of scrolls

28

exists in Yunii. I went there once. But whatever knowledge they have, they guard jealously."

"But magic can do so much good. Why didn't they share the knowledge?"

"Magic is not good, Maria. It just *is*. People who want to do dark magic, people who want to do evil, will. A year or so before I went to Yunii, a magic scroll was stolen by a young apprentice shaman from Reune, a country west of the Thundrous Mountains. Since then, all the scrolls were put into one place, and only the red-robed magician-lords of Yunii are allowed to see them. Those magicians, Maria, are much more powerful than magicians of the First Order. They understand how to teach everyone with talent to use the magic in the way that suits them, not in the way that suits their teachers. When I told the Council what I had discovered, they refused to believe. So I resigned from the Order. When Yunii attacks us, riding with their soldiers will be their full magicians."

Whatever Maria was going to say was cut off by the sounds of yelling men and pounding hooves. Tristan jumped up and grabbed his sling while Lin went to the door. Bursting though the trees and nearing the cottage, Maria saw nine riders. Three had lit torches and five carried bows notched with arrows. The last man, riding behind the rest, carried no weapons, and instead of a soldier's leather vest, wore a red robe.

Lin grabbed Tristan and spun him around. "A full magician-lord from Yunii! Take Maria out the window and run for the forest. When Tristan hesitated and moved closer to Lin, Lin pushed him toward Maria. "Do what I say, boy! There's no reason for three of us to die if only one has to. And I won't die easily!" Lin stepped out the door and shouted a spell Maria had never heard. She looked back just as Tristan lifted her out the window and saw the lead riders' horses slam into an invisible wall Lin had created. Arrows from the other riders hit the wall and bounced harmlessly to the ground.

All the invaders were in front of the house so Tristan and Maria were able to slip out of the window unseen. Maria pulled Tristan's hand. "We can't leave Tiny tied up."

Tristan tilted his head slightly to look into Maria's eyes. Then he nodded and crawled along the ground next to the cottage. When he reached the rope, he pulled on it until the badly frightened donkey came to him. Tristan took the halter off and Tiny ran away. Maria heard a deep voice calling from the front of the house.

"A true magician. I never expected to find someone who could create the wall living in the middle of nowhere. Very few people outside of Yunii know the spell."

"There are many things about us you don't know," said Lin.

The deep voice laughed. "Do you think Kestra's Order of Magicians can stop us? Watch your wall." The voice mumbled something Maria couldn't make out. "Your wall is gone, old man."

Tristan had now returned to Maria, but instead of running, he pulled her back to the house. He held her hand tightly as they stood silently, listening.

"Fire your arrows into the roof of the building," said the deep voice. "Try to stop them, old man."

Again, Maria heard Lin speak an unknown spell, and,

immediately afterward, she heard several "thuds" as arrows struck the cottage.

The deep voice laughed again. "What we don't know about your Order of Magicians is not worth knowing. We need your country, old man, for it blocks our way. Our king will be emperor of the four nations."

Lin began to recite a spell as Tristan grabbed Maria's hand and ran.

"Two of them are getting away!" someone shouted. The Yuniian magician began to chant; the cottage suddenly exploded. Tristan pushed Maria down and covered her body with his own.

When Maria looked up, where the cottage had stood was nothing but charred ash. Of the nine men that had attacked, only the three farthest from the door remained. The other six, and their mounts, had vanished. The Yuniian magician staggered forward with blood pouring out of a huge cut in his forehead. His eyes were wide open, and even from a distance, Maria could see the surprised expression on his face. The magician-lord tried to raise an arm, but it never lifted more than a few inches. He crumpled like a thrown rag doll.

The two remaining soldiers notched their bows and fired. Tristan rolled before the arrows struck, jumped up, pulling Maria after him, and ran.

By the time they reached the trees, Tristan had taken a stone from his pocket and put it into his leather sling. He whirled it quickly in a wide circle — the lead horse entered the woods and Tristan fired. The rock crashed into the rider's head. Even before he fell, another stone was swinging. But this time, the second man ducked and the stone went over his head.

The soldier dropped his bow, pulled a sword, and charged. Tristan lifted himself onto a branch as the horse approached and jumped, hitting the soldier. As they both plunged down, Tristan grabbed the soldier's knife and stabbed it deep into the man's side. Tristan rose, quickly running to the other soldier and listening to his heart. That man too, was dead. The youth moved away from the body and sat leaning against a tree.

Maria went to him. When he looked up, Maria saw red in his eyes, but no tears. She didn't know what to do or say. So she sat next to him and they both listened to the now silent woods.

Chapter 4

The sun began to set and still Tristan sat, face down, eyes staring in front of him. He rocked ever so slightly while rubbing his hands over his arms. Every time Maria spoke, his head turned a little, but after a moment he went back to looking at the ground.

Maria got up and walked to the edge of the clearing. Whatever had been in the cottage, including her belongings, was now part of the black ash covering the ground. She called Tiny's name, but the donkey didn't return. On the way back to Tristan, she brought the horses of the dead soldiers. After unsaddling and tying them to a tree, Maria looked in the saddlebags and found some food — enough to last a few days — a small pouch of coins — some from Kestra and some from Yunii — a few knives, and a change of clothing for each man.

She put the bags next to Tristan and began collecting wood for a fire. She moved slowly — she had things to think about. Though she had only just met Lin, she had liked him and knew that if he had lived, he might have been able to teach her how to use the magic she so desperately wanted. But he was gone. *Where will I go now? I have nothing, I have no one.*

When the wood was ready, she kneeled before it, crossed her arms over her chest, and whispered the spell that would start a fire.

> "Yo-URAY woenetter SOMber
> Yo-uray woeNETTER somBER."

Nothing happened. *I have to relax!* She recited her calming spell and waited until her heart slowed. "Now it will work.

> "Yo-URAY woenetter SOMber
> Yo-uray woeNETTER somBER."

Again, nothing happened. "Why aren't you burning!" she shouted at the wood. "I said the words *right!*"

Tristan got up, violently pushing Maria aside. It was getting dark now. The sun was almost gone and the twin moons had not yet appeared. But even in the dim light, Maria could see the hard stare on his face. His lips were tight, his hands balled into fists. He looked at the wood and closed his eyes for a second. When they opened, flames sprang up from the branches. Maria had to scurry back.

She stared at him. "You have to say the magic to get it to work. You have to *say the words*. Eonoway told me. You can't ... But you did ..." All of a sudden, tears flowed. "I told Lin I was no magician. I told him the magic won't listen to me. Everyone who ever called me a misfit apprentice was right. I can't do it, Tristan." Maria sat next to

34

the fire and began to cry hysterically. All the frustration she had felt since her first failure as an apprentice swelled up inside her. All the whispers she had never let hurt her, hurt her now. She tried to stop, but her chest moved in and out as her sobs disappeared into the night.

Maria became aware of a pair of hands holding her wrists. When she looked up, she saw Tristan's face. The cold stare was gone, and for the first time since they met, he smiled. He put her hands together and lifted them to his chest over his heart. Maria felt that that was his way of apologizing. He sat next to the fire and motioned her to join him. In the dirt, Tristan drew a rectangle with a hole in it. When she looked at him, he pointed toward the clearing.

"I forgot what Lin told me, didn't I?" She wiped her eyes with her sleeves and smiled. "The magic won't mold itself to me. I have to find my own way. I have to get my words through the magic hole, as Lin said. That's what you want to tell me, isn't it?"

Tristan nodded. Then he waved his hand over the fire, and instantly it went out.

"How did you do that?" But Tristan said nothing. Maria moved closer to him in the now dark forest. Neither Bern nor Pern appeared over the treeline and the forest was bathed in black shadows. Maria closed her eyes and tried again.

"Yo-uray woenetter somber."

The wood still did not burn. In the darkness, she felt Tristan's hand touch hers. He took one of her fingers and traced a large wedge on the ground. Then, with his other hand, he hit the ground over the wedge.

"I have to do the magic my own way, don't I? I have to start from the beginning and see what works." *But how? How can I teach myself what Eonoway couldn't?* She noisily let out a deep breath. She tried to remember the first time she had heard the spell, tried to remember which words felt unnatural to her. Eonoway had yelled when Maria had changed them, reminding her that the pattern of spell-making can never be changed. Maria thought back and said the words silently in her mind before speaking them out loud.

"Yo-ray woeneeter sombear."

The flame reappeared. "I did it, Tristan! Maria jumped at him and held him in a tight hug. But when he didn't return it, she let go. She reached into the travel pack of one of the soldiers and pulled out two journey cakes. As they ate, she looked at him. "I'm sorry about Lin. You lost a father, and I lost someone who could have given me a new life. I have to forget what Eonoway taught me and learn it again on my own. But without Lin to tell me what to do, it's going to be impossible. I only remember the simple spells, and without my spell book I'll never remember the harder ones." She picked up a twig and rubbed it between her palms. Then she took a deep breath. "Tristan, can I stay with you for a while? I don't have anywhere else to go."

Tristan didn't answer. He just looked at her with the same expressionless stare he usually wore.

In the morning, Maria walked back to the clearing to see if any of her belongings had survived Lin's magic. Holding the bottom of her dress up, she moved the ashes around with her foot. She had almost given up when she kicked something solid. She knelt down and brushed the ash away. "Tristan! Tristan!" she called, running to the woods. "Come here!"

In a few seconds, he appeared, leading the two horses. Maria ran to him, took his hand, and started running back to the ash pile. Tristan was reluctant to follow, but Maria held on tightly. "Look," she said, as they stood in the ashes.

Tristan lowered his head. Eyes wide, he dropped to his knees and furiously began wiping ashes off what looked like a large block of solid glass. When the ashes were completely gone, Maria could see Lin's body. It was lying flat — eyes closed, a half smile on his face — frozen within the slab of glass. Tristan placed his hands on the end of the glass and pushed. The block moved, but only a few inches. He looked at Maria and pointed to the clearing, away from the ashes. Maria knelt down, and the two managed to slide the glass onto the grass. Tristan pointed to Maria and then to Lin. He opened his hand and lowered it, palm down.

"You want me to stay here?"

He nodded. Still half covered with black ash, he ran to one of the horses, jumped on, and raced off.

Maria reached for the pocket that she had always kept her spell book in, but stopped before her hand touched the edge of her dress. *I can't do anything. Even if I knew what Lin did, even if I had my spell book, I still wouldn't be able to do anything.* She went back to the horse and tied it to a tree. Then she brushed as much of the ash off her dress as she could and walked beyond the clearing, looking for the stream Lin had told Tristan to wash in. She quickly found it, drank, washed the ash from her face and hands, and went back to Lin. Several hours later, she started a small fire near the imprisoned magician and ate. It was past noon before anything happened.

Maria heard a low rumbling sound coming from the woods. Something was racing through the forest toward her. In a minute she saw Tristan. His horse was foaming and white lather covered its chest. Behind him, breaking through the last line of trees, Maria saw a wagon. Driving it, a stern, set look on her roundish face, was a plump, middle-aged woman with grayish hair. She pulled hard on the reins and stopped the wagon next to Maria's fire. Tristan was already out of the saddle and kneeling next to Lin. The woman joined him.

Maria took Tristan's horse and unsaddled it. Using a shirt from the saddle bag, she wiped it down. Then she walked it around the clearing while Tristan and the woman ignored her and examined Lin's glass coffin. After a few minutes Maria led the horse to the stream and let it drink.

On her return to the clearing, Maria saw Tristan banging a rock against the glass and the woman sitting by the fire. For the first time, she noticed Maria and motioned for the girl to come sit by her. Maria did so, and while Tristan continued hitting the glass, the woman spoke.

"It's going to take Tristan a few minutes to work his anger out. It won't do Lin any good, but then again it won't do him any harm, either. While we wait, why don't we get acquainted. My name is Befany. I'm a colleague of Lin's. Who are you?"

"My name is Maria Ronlin."

"All right, Maria. Start from the beginning and tell me what happened."

Maria began from the time Tristan had saved her. She didn't get far when Befany motioned for her to stop. "Why were you going to Deventap?"

Maria hesitated a bit, then started over. This time, she began when Eonoway had told her to leave. Befany listened to the rest without any interruption.

Befany rose. On the other side of the clearing, she saw the body of the Yuniian magician and went to it. She looked in the robe's pockets but returned empty handed. By this time, Tristan had tired himself out and joined Maria by the fire. He added more wood and watched the flames go higher.

"What did Lin do?" asked Maria.

"I'm not sure," Befany answered. "The first spell was one that we discovered by accident and never used again. Lin created a bubble of light, like the one you used to find Tristan the first time you saw him. Only this bubble destroyed everything within it. Lin didn't take the chance of waiting until the bubble moved far enough away from him so he would be safe. He ordered it to destruct while he was still within its light."

"But the glass case?" asked Maria.

"I don't know. We never talked about anything like that. I'm sure the Yuniian magician didn't do it, so Lin must have done it to himself."

Tristan turned around suddenly and stared at Befany.

39

"That's right, Tristan," said Befany. "He must have done it to save his life."

Tristan put his hands together and then spread them up and out.

"I don't know how to open the glass." When Tristan stood and started walking toward his horse, Befany called after him. "Running off won't help Lin. Besides, we've got to get him back to my cottage. Once there, we can talk about ways to free him."

Maria saw his back rise and fall as he took a deep breath. Then his head nodded up and down.

It took the three of them several tries to finally lift the glass coffin into the wagon. Then Maria and Tristan followed as Befany drove home. It was late afternoon by the time they had left the trees and entered a long, flat plain. Maria saw many farmers walking behind their horses as the animals pulled wooden plows through the soil. The spring planting had begun and they would work until dark. Several of the men stopped and watched the three pass, but no one waved or called out a greeting.

Befany came to a dirt road and followed a sign pointing to Deventap, but after a mile or so, she turned onto a small path. In a few minutes, they came to a house built on the edge of either a very small lake or a very large pond.

"We have to get Lin into the house," said Befany. "We'll put him in the small room next to the kitchen."

Maria helped them slide the glass coffin off the wagon, and the three managed to carry it up the few steps and into the house. Then she followed Befany and Tristan into a cluttered room just off the hallway. Tristan sat on the floor while Befany sat in an old, worn chair and pointed to a newer one. Maria sat.

"Tristan," Befany said, touching him on the shoulder, "Lin saved himself from the backlash of his spell by using magic. We've often told you, for every spell, there's a counterspell. All we have to do is find it. Why don't you get some wood from the box on the porch and start the fire? All of a sudden there's a chill in the air."

Maria watched him leave. "Befany, last night, when I couldn't get the fire spell to work, Tristan did it. Who is he? How come he can use the magic without saying the words?"

Befany shook her head. "I don't know who he is. Neither did Lin. He and I were never able to find out who was responsible for Tristan or who hurt him. Whenever Lin and I were together discussing magic, he was always with us. He can read and has read our spell books. He's very bright and for all I know he's even memorized the scroll we also possess."

"You have a scroll! Can I see it? I've never seen a real scroll. Eonoway only had copies."

Befany got up and took a scroll case from the shelf. Carefully, she pulled out a yellowed scroll and unrolled it on the table top. It was small, about eighteen inches long.

"What does it say?" asked Maria.

"I don't know, child. Once, when I was in the Order of Magicians . . ."

"You, too! Were you also a Magician of the First Order?"

"Before I met Lin I was. Then I got to believing what he

said about how magic is taught and left the Order when he did. Lin and I found this in the ruins of an old castle. Neither of us understood it. It's written in the same language as the other scrolls and we've pronounced all of the words in various combinations. Nothing's ever happened."

"What's that?" asked Maria, leaning over the table and staring.

In the center of the scroll was a small picture. It looked to Maria like a door framed with circles, and, in each of the circles, was another tiny picture. She couldn't make them out, but they appeared to be animals. The only thing she could tell was that in each circular picture were two green dots.

"I have no idea," said Befany as she rolled the scroll up. "I've never seen anything like that before."

"What about Tristan?" asked Maria. "Can he do anything with the words on the scroll?"

"No," answered Befany as she sat. "There's something strange about the magic Tristan does. Some spells, like the fire spell, work very easily for him. Unlike most magicians who sometimes have trouble doing magic, those spells work all the time for him. But there are other spells he can't do, no matter how hard he tries. Lin and I both believed that if we discovered how Tristan does it, we could learn something very important about how magic works."

"But how can he do it without speaking?"

"I don't know. All I know is he can do magic, and that has taught us, and now you, that no matter what we think we know, we don't know everything. We still have much to learn. If only . . ."

Tristan appeared in the doorway carrying several logs.

42

He put them in the fireplace and soon the sounds of crackling wood filled the tiny room. "Come here, children," said Befany, sitting back. Maria got off the chair and joined Tristan on the floor. "When I saw Lin this afternoon, I spoke every spell I knew that might have been able to break the magic that imprisons him. Nothing I did helped."

Tristan turned away and faced the fire, but Befany leaned forward, cupped her hand under his chin, and turned his face toward her. "I didn't say I was giving up. Now listen, Tristan, you know how much I care for Lin, don't you?" When Tristan nodded, Befany's hand moved up and down with his chin. "I promise I will do everything I can to break the spell."

Maria watched Tristan stare into Befany's eyes for a few seconds before he pulled his head away.

"Maria, what are your plans?"

"I don't have any. I asked Tristan if I could stay with him last night and I think he said yes."

"Tristan, I have never lied to you and I won't start now. I don't know enough to help Lin. I don't think any Magician of the First Order knows enough. But I know where that information might be. The trouble is, getting there and back will be very dangerous. I would go with you, but these old bones of mine would never be able to cross the mountains."

Tristan stood up quickly. He looked around the room and when he saw an old short sword, he went to it. He returned, standing before Befany with the sword in his hand. Then, he turned to Maria.

"He wants to know if you still want to go with him?"

"Where's he going?"

"I want you both to go to Yunii. I want you to try to break into the magician's library in their capital city, Casgarn, and steal as many scrolls as you can. Maybe we'll be lucky and in one of them I'll find something to break the spell."

"But . . . but how can I help him? I couldn't even put four thieves to sleep."

"I don't know," answered Befany. "But two people, working together, can often do things one person can't."

"But Tristan," said Maria, turning to face him, "you saw what happened when I tried the magic. You'd end up taking care of me half the time. All I'd be is a tagalong. You can't really want me to go?"

Tristan looked at her. Then he touched her arm once before turning and adding more wood to the fire.

"All right," she whispered. "I'll go if you want me to. But I think you're making a big mistake."

Chapter 5

They left the next morning. Maria rode alongside Tristan as they headed north and slightly west, toward the town of Ventor. Maria understood why Befany had told them to go there because she remembered Enoway's geography lessons. The land of the four nations resembled a large bone. Yunii, the largest country, was the top. The middle narrow part was Kestra. The bottom was divided into Mikloner and Ekloy. That's what the Yuniian magician meant when he said they needed Kestra. If Helborat wanted to be emperor of the four nations, he had to conquer Kestra first.

In the west, the Thundrous Mountains ran from the top of Yunii to the bottom of Mikloner. In the east, from the top of Yunii to the end of Ekloy, was the Thousand Mile Desert.

"It's too dangerous to enter Yunii from central Kestra," Befany told them. "That border is closed due to the war everyone is sure will happen. I want you to go the long way. Go to Ventor, the northwestern-most village in Kestra. From there, enter the Thundrous Mountains and make your way north. Just be careful. Yunii patrols are

45

using the same route to sneak into Kestra. You don't want to run into any of them."

It would take almost two weeks to reach Ventor, so Tristan set a brisk pace. He camped early the first day and motioned for Maria to join him when the wood was ready. He pointed to it and then to her.

"You want me to start it?"

He just looked at her and went off with his sling held loosely in his hand.

I can do this, she thought after he had gone. *I can make a fire.* She stood next to the wood, looked down at it, and said,

"Yo-URAY woenetter SOMber,"

and waited, and waited, and waited. *It worked last time!*

"Yo-URAY woenetter SOMber!"

she yelled. It still didn't work. "What's wrong with me! Why can't I do it! It's a simple spell." By now, her heart was pumping quickly, a lump was in her throat, and her eyes had begun to sting. She closed them and recited her calming spell. *At least that one always works,* she thought as she relaxed. She sat down and took the magician's pose. But as her palms touched her shoulders, she remembered what Lin had told her. Closing her eyes and thinking, but keeping her arms crossed, she whispered again.

"Yo-ray woeneeter sombear."

46

Wood crackled and when she open her eyes, the fire was burning. *I have to remember to fit my words to the magic. I have to start all over with my spells and teach myself. But how can I do that? Why did that have to happen to Lin? He could have taught me to be a magician.*

Half an hour later, Tristan returned carrying a plump duck. An hour later, they were eating. Though Befany had given them enough supplies to last a long time, Tristan preferred to catch their dinner when he could.

Avoiding the tiny towns on the way, they continued to Ventor, and on the thirteenth day from Befany's cottage they reached the village. They quickly found the only inn and, after a few moments of haggling about the price, arranged to stay there before heading into the mountains. Maria then told the man to add two coppers so they could each take a bath. The owner said four, if they used the same water. Tristan held up three fingers and made a motion of dumping water. The innkeeper said seven, but when Maria put six coppers on the counter and said, "Two hot baths with clean water," the man took the money.

That evening, as they sat in a corner of the common room eating a meal of stew and bread, they heard people talking and caught up on the news. Helborat had invaded Kestra nine days before, driving his army through central Kestra. The rider who came with the message had called for all men to mount and ride to defend their country. The first battle had been a disaster. The Yuniian magicians that rode with Helborat's army easily helped their soldiers defeat Andraya's forces. The men who were standing at the bar told each other why they couldn't go now or spoke of the future when they would.

Tristan didn't look up as he finished eating, but Maria saw how tightly he held his fork. He was angry that these men who could fight, wouldn't.

"Don't be too hard on them," she whispered. "If too many men leave there won't be enough left to work the fields. Next winter, everyone will be hungry. My father was a farmer, so I know."

Just then, two of the men who were arguing began to push each other and raise their voices. "You're just a coward, Okrim. Everyone knows that your brothers are too young to fight, but they're old enough to do the farm work."

"Are they old enough to use this?" Okrim yelled back, pulling out his knife. "Who's going to protect the family if I'm gone!"

"Protect them from whom? From us?" The first man spread his arms out pointing to the other men in the room.

"I don't see *your* travel bag packed and ready, Horro," said Okrim.

Horro spit on the floor. "You know there's just me to work my land. Would you have my wife and baby starve while I'm off protecting Kestra so that cowards like you can stay and hide under their beds!"

Okrim jumped, raising his knife and trying to plunge it into Horro's chest. Horro grabbed Okrim's descending wrist and the two fell forward.

Though some of the men cheered one or the other fighter, several of them managed to separate the two. Everyone was hollering, and it took several minutes for the room to quiet down enough so the innkeeper's voice could be heard.

"That's enough of that. I won't have any killing in my place, understand, Okrim?"

"But he called me a coward. You all know I'm not, don't you?" Some of the men nodded while others shook their heads. "Do you see what you've done?" Okrim screamed at Horro. "These are my friends, and now you've turned them against me. I won't forget this. I . . ." He stopped when he saw Maria and Tristan. He pushed his way through the men and stopped at their table.

"You," he said, pointing at Tristan. "You're a stranger so you have no side to take. Would you call a man a coward because he chooses to protect his family?"

Tristan looked up, but as always remained silent.

"Are you siding with him, then?" Okrim said, putting both hands on the table and leaning close to Tristan's face.

"Come on, boy." One of the men crowding around the table spoke up. "You don't have to be afraid. Say what you want."

"He doesn't talk," said Maria.

"Doesn't or won't. Or are you calling me a coward, too?"

Maria saw Tristan's hand pull back and was afraid he would reach for his knife. All they wanted when they came to the common room was a hot meal before going to sleep. Now they were in the middle of an argument that had nothing to do with them. Maria's pulse beat quicker as their table, pushed by the men, inched closer, forcing her to move her chair back against the wall. She reached over and held Tristan's hand. "I told you," she said, standing, "he can't talk."

"Then you tell me," said Okrim. "You heard what Horro said. Who's lying?"

"That's right," called Horro over the crowd, "bully a young girl into saying what you want. You're very brave, Okrim. If Helborat ever attacks Ventor with an army of children, I bet you'll be the first one to defend us."

Okrim stepped to the edge of the table, and with a quick sweeping movement of his arm, pushed Maria past him and onto the floor. "Then you tell me," he shouted at Tristan.

Tristan sprang up, throwing the table into the faces of the men nearest to it. His knife was out. He pushed several men who were between him and Maria out of the way and grabbed Maria while stepping toward the wall. Okrim pulled his knife and came at them.

Maria swallowed hard and ignored a pain starting in her stomach. She had to do something now — their lives depended on it. *Work, please work!*

"In no lu-ter!"

she shouted, as her hand flew across her chest. Her eyes closed; she concentrated, not on the words, but on the magic. The magic came. The magic listened.

"In no lu-ter.
In no lu-ter!"

Suddenly, the room was deathly quiet. The spell she cast froze everyone except Tristan. This was a strange spell, for when it worked, everyone who heard it was unable to move as long as it was chanted. Everyone, that is, except the people the magician didn't want to be frozen. No one knew why the spell worked in this selective way; it just did.

When Maria stopped speaking, the spell broke, but the men remained motionless. Though Maria wasn't wearing the brown robe of a lesser magician, only those trained as magicians could do magic. All of a sudden, Maria was someone special — she was the eyes and voice of Queen Andraya. She stepped toward Okrim, who tried to back up but couldn't. His way was blocked by the men staring at Maria. As she stood next to Okrim, Maria thought everyone in the room could tell how frightened she was because her heart was beating so loudly. But she had to finish what she had started. She recited her calming spell and waited for the lump in her throat to go away. *Please,* she thought to the magic, *Please.* Before crossing her arms, she pushed her palms against her stomach, hoping that would stop the empty feeling that was moving inside her. It didn't, so she swallowed and made an "X" with her arms across her chest. *What if it doesn't work? What will I do then . . . no, it has to work.*

"Remember Okrim, you brought this on yourself. We just wanted to be left alone. Tell these men, why are you still in Ventor? Why are you not helping to protect our land?" She closed her eyes and tried desperately to remember the truth spell. She mouthed the words to herself, and when they sounded right, she said them half aloud. In all the time she had apprenticed with Eonoway, this spell had worked only once for her.

"Eewow gerinta sinkrata discot."

Okrim lowered his arms. A glazed look covered his eyes as he stared straight ahead. When he spoke, his voice was a dead monotone. "There . . . will . . . not . . . be . . . e . . . nough . . . food . . . this . . . win . . . ter . . . my . . . fam . . . i . . . ly . . . is . . . far . . . ming . . . all . . . the . . . land . . . we . . . own . . . plus . . . sev . . . er . . . al . . . o . . . ther . . . pla . . . ces . . . not . . . owned . . . by . . . an . . . y . . . one . . . when . . . har . . . vest . . . comes . . . peo . . . ple . . . will . . . pay . . . a . . . great . . . deal . . . for . . . food . . . my . . . fam . . . i . . . ly . . . will . . . be . . . come . . . rich." The faraway look from his eyes vanished.

"That's not . . ." Okrim started.

"One cannot lie under a truth spell," said the man next to Okrim, spitting in his face. "A coward is one thing. But a man who robs his friends to become rich while others die to protect him is no better than dirt." He held Okrim by the shirt and threw him toward the door. Before Okrim left, he turned; there was a look of hate in his face, and he stared a long time at Maria before walking out.

Everyone backed away from Maria as the innkeeper pushed his way before her. She held Tristan's arm tightly; her legs felt weak.

"Who are you?" the innkeeper asked.

"I am Maria Ronlin, former apprentice to Eonoway, Magician of the First Order, Counselor to the Queen."

"If you are a lesser magician, why aren't you wearing a brown robe?"

Maria didn't name herself a lesser magician. The innkeeper did. She didn't want to lie if she could help it. "All my belongings were destroyed when a full magician from Yunii attacked the people I was with."

Maria hoped the innkeeper wouldn't question her any further. He looked at her and lowered his head. "Welcome, Maria Ronlin, Lesser Magician, voice of Queen Andraya. Rest with us in peace." When he gave Maria the ritual greeting, he accepted her for what he thought she was, a full lesser magician, and though a young girl, one who spoke for the queen herself.

Chapter 6

Maria slept soundly, but in the twilight hours of early morning, something aroused her. She groggily opened an eye and listened. Everything seemed normal. No one else was in the room except Tristan, sleeping on the floor. The only sound she heard, other than some chickens clucking in the courtyard below, was Tristan's breathing. She closed her eye and pulled the blanket up to her neck. But she couldn't sleep.

She sat and searched the room carefully. Again, everything was the way it should be. *What's wrong!* She took a deep breath as she lay back down, and that's when she smelled it. A faint odor — smoke.

Instantly she was up, waking Tristan. "Something's burning," she said when his eyes opened. Maria was amazed at how quickly he was fully awake. In half a minute, he was standing, the short sword Befany gave him strapped to his side, and their packs in his hands. When she opened the door, smoke was in the hallway.

"Fire! Fire!" she yelled as she banged on each door. "Get out! Get out!" Tristan pulled her as he ran for the stairs, but by the time they reached them, flames were racing up the stairwell. They backed up toward their room while Maria continued to bang on the doors. "We're trapped! Jump out the windows!"

Smoke was now pooling on the ceiling and Maria had to bend to breathe. It was getting hard to see; Tristan led her into their room and to the open window. He lifted her up and lowered her out. She fell several feet to the ground but was unhurt. He jumped down after.

By now, the entire bottom floor was in flames. People jumped out windows; smoke flooded from the building. Tristan was leading Maria away from the flames when an arrow flew out of the darkness, missing her head by inches and striking the wall of the burning inn. Tristan roughly pushed Maria down and, pulling his sword, raced off toward the woods in the direction the arrow had come from. Almost immediately after that, Maria felt hands picking her up. It was the innkeeper, and he stood between her and the trees.

"Let's get out of the open," he said, as villagers appeared carrying buckets of water. He raised his voice and called out. "It's no use. We can't save it." Someone handed him half an arrow. He took it and led Maria to the nearest building. Once inside, the man looked at the arrow. "Okrim's mark," he said and spat on the floor. "His family will pay for this. You are witness," he said to Maria. "Okrim burned my inn, and if you hadn't woken us, we all could have died. I claim queen's justice. As Andraya's voice, you must deed to me all that Okrim's family owns to pay for rebuilding my inn."

Tristan appeared in the doorway, and when everyone looked at him, he shook his head.

"Don't worry. We'll find him. Well, Magician, what does the queen say to my claim?"

Maria was trapped. Whatever she said would be written down by the village record keeper. Only a true magician could speak for the queen and she was no magician. But she had to say something or else the people would accuse her of not belonging to the Order of Magicians. That would mean she practiced dark magic, a crime punishable by death.

Tristan must have understood her dilemma for he came and stood next to her. He took the arrow from the inn-keeper, handing it to another man. That man examined the markings just below the feathers and nodded. "It's Okrim's, all right. I'll swear to it." Several other men looked at the arrow and each said the same.

Maria recited her calming spell. *What would Eonoway do? She'd give the innkeeper everything Okrim's family owns, just as he asked. But that's not fair. Eonoway would do exactly what the law says, but that's still not fair. I've got to do something else.* She took a deep breath and inched closer to Tristan.

"Rebuild your inn the way it was. Let Okrim's family pay for it. Let them pay for your upkeep while your inn is rebuilt. Let them also pay for what was lost by the people staying in the inn. But I ask you, since they didn't know what Okrim did, leave them their farm so they won't starve. For the sake of his parents and younger brothers, let them pay you over the next year or two. You have the right to ask for everything." She paused a moment to think. "Helborat will cause enough suffering in Kestra. We shouldn't cause more on our own people."

Tristan slid his hand down Maria's arm and squeezed her hand.

The innkeeper stared at Maria without saying anything. Then he looked out the door as his inn collapsed. When he turned back, he nodded his head. "That is fair, Maria Ronlin, lesser magician and voice of the queen.

"Lenard," he called out, "you heard what the magician said. Record it and send word to Okrim's parents that their son is now an outlaw. They will have two years to pay the debts this night has cost. If they do not, then all their land is mine. Is that not so?" he asked Maria. She nodded her head. "So said the voice of Queen Andraya."

Tristan picked up his travel-pack and handed Maria hers. Then he pointed to the mountains through the window; the sun had just begun to light the distant peaks. He wanted to go, but the villagers wouldn't let them. An hour later when they did leave, each carried a new and fully stuffed travel-pack. The innkeeper, and the other people staying at the inn, insisted on providing them with everything they could carry, including a large cowhide that could be used to make a lean-to. The innkeeper told them that they would have to leave their horses behind because the animals could not cross the mountains. "And be careful," he had said as they left. "Summer storms can be fierce in those mountains."

"We will," answered Maria. "And thank you."

"No, Magician," he answered, "thank you." He bowed slightly as the two left.

"He called me a magician, Tristan. Wait a minute! What happens if another magician comes to Ventor and reads what I did in the village records? What if the Order of Magicians finds out I passed judgment on someone? What will they do? They might accuse me of using dark magic."

Stepping in front of her, Tristan tapped her lightly on her temple as he pretended to lower a hood over her head.

"A magician's hood? Are you saying I'm going to be a magician one day?"

Tristan nodded.

"But how? I couldn't even stop one man from burning an inn. I told you . . . Tristan, how can I help you steal anything from a library guarded by Yuniian magicians?"

Tristan shook his head and gave her one of his rare smiles. Then he turned and headed toward the mountains.

The magic worked for me twice. But why? What did I do differently? And why didn't I sense the fire earlier? Eonoway would have. Why couldn't I? If I were a better magician, I could have saved the inn. There are spells that put out fires. All I did was declare Okrim guilty and tell . . . what WILL happen if the Order of Magicians finds out I used magic and spoke for the queen? Will they accuse me of using dark magic? Maria remained as silent as Tristan.

Five days later they were deep in the mountains. The road had vanished and they made their own trail as they climbed the forested slopes. Yunii was north of them, but the innkeeper had told them that the easiest way was not north, but west. "After four or five days," he said, "you'll see two peaks. You can't miss them; they're the tallest ones in this part of the Thundrous Mountains. Head for them. A day or so farther west you'll come to a valley that goes north. Stay in that valley until the end. Then you'll see several trails that head back east. They all lead to Yunii. It will take you about a week and a half longer than if you go into the mountains and head north, but you'll avoid climbing over some dangerous ground."

Maria guessed that Tristan took the advice because he kept leading them westward. In the early afternoon, Tristan stopped. Staring at the darkening clouds growing in the western sky, he motioned for Maria to get some wood. While she was gone, he untied the cowhide and secured the ends of it to several trees he found growing in a clump near the rocky mountainside. That finished, he covered the hide with layers of branches from nearby trees. On her second try, Maria started a small fire under the edge of the lean-to, and when the first drops of rain started to fall, they moved to the back of the shelter.

Thunder began to rumble in the distance, and with each new clap it became louder and louder. Rain that had started gently suddenly pounded into their lean-to as if it resented something stopping it from hitting the ground. The cowhide flapped so violently that twice Tristan had to leave the shelter to test the knots holding it to the trees. Every time the wind blew water under the lip of the lean-to, the fire hissed, forcing Tristan to use a thick branch to slide the whole fire farther away from the opening. The storm raged into the evening before it moved off. The downpour became a drizzle, and by the time the twin moons poked their heads into the sky, only wispy clouds blew over the tiny camp. By morning, the summer sun had already dried most of the ground.

Maria was sitting by a small fire waiting for Tristan, who had gone to hunt their breakfast. A twig snapped — silence — then another snap. Someone was doing a poor job of sneaking up on her. Maria knew it wasn't Tristan. Quickly she looked around and ran for cover. Just as she reached the trees holding the lean-to, a loud thud exploded near her head, then the twanging sound of an arrow vibrating in something solid.

"Tristan!" she shouted, wedging herself into the space between trees and mountainside. "Tristan!"

A second arrow whizzed past; this time it missed the trees and bounced off a rock.

Use your magic! Quickly, she crossed her arms and whispered the words of a protection spell that should have stopped the third arrow from lodging in a tree several feet away. "What else?" she said to herself.

> "Me HA-da keynote eesTAR bremTO.
> ME ha-da KEYnote EEStar BREMto.
> Me ha-DA keyNOTE EESTAR bremto."

Slowly, a bubble of light grew around her and floated up through the trees into the clearing beyond. The seeking spell did not prevent the next arrow from coming closer to her, but it would let her see where the archer was hiding. She watched, keeping her arms pressed closely to her chest, as the bubble stopped and changed direction. The person was moving.

She couldn't think of another spell, and when she lowered her arms, the bubble disappeared. *If I had been a better apprentice, Eonoway would have taught me spells to fight with. Where's Tristan!*

She saw him — Okrim. He had just left the rock he had

been hiding behind. Holding a long knife whose blade shone in the sun, he ran straight for Maria.

> "In no lu-ter!
> In no lu-ter!"

But Okrim didn't stop and Maria knew why. Wrapped around his head and covering his ears were several strips of cloth. The freezing spell only worked if you could hear it.

"You cost me everything! I can never go home now. But before I leave Kestra forever, I want to know you'll never go home either."

Maria's eyes darted like a frightened mouse. If she could keep the trees between Okrim and herself, she might be able to hold him off until Tristan returned. But Okrim lunged for her. Without magic, all she could do to save herself was run, and she raced for the clearing.

She had reached the edge of it when she heard a scream. Turning, she saw a large cat raking its claws over Okrim's face. The knife dropped — Okrim staggered back. The cat jumped away as Okrim lifted his hands. Blood flowed down his cheeks; his head swung sideways as he tried to focus his eyes. He saw Maria. Wiping his face with one arm, he picked up his knife and charged again.

The cat attacked once more. This time, it leaped on the man's back, ripping both cloth and flesh as it slid down. Okrim screamed and twisted his body, throwing the cat off. The knife whooshed out, slicing air, missing the animal. As he faced Maria again, Okrim's head snapped back. A gash opened on his forehead; he fell to his knees. Maria spied Tristan, sling in hand, running. When he reached her, she wrapped her arms around him. Together they watched Okrim sway back and forth holding his head in his hands. Blood dripped through his fingers, and pulling the cloth off his ears, he pressed it against his face.

Tristan broke away from Maria and picked up the knife Okrim had dropped. Next he reached behind Okrim and pulled out the arrows left in the quiver. Maria watched Tristan break them over his knee. While Okrim was still kneeling holding his bleeding head, Tristan followed footprints to the rock Okrim had hidden behind. He reached down and picked up a bow. He broke that too and angrily threw the pieces at Okrim on his way back to Maria. Then he took Maria's hand and led her to the fire. He covered it with dirt, removed the cowhide, and picked up their packs. Holding everything in his arms, and without looking back, he left.

Maria walked next to him half-dazed. A few minutes later, Tristan stopped next to a dead rabbit tied to a branch. He began packing their belongings; Maria said her calming spell. When she was ready, she spoke. "I can't stay with you anymore, Tristan."

He stopped and looked at her.

"Don't you understand? I can't help you. I can't even help myself. Eonoway wouldn't be afraid of a whole company of soldiers and I couldn't even protect myself against one man with cloth in his ears. We'll get killed if we stay together because instead of taking care of yourself you'll be taking care of me. I care about you, Tristan, and I don't want you to die. Let me go back to Kestra. You don't need me."

Tristan went to her, gently turned her around so she faced west, and continued walking. Maria followed, her stomach still churning.

Half an hour later, Tristan stopped, motioned for her to make a fire, and began to prepare the rabbit that still hung over his shoulders. While their breakfast was roasting over the flames, Maria heard a meow. Walking toward them from the surrounding trees, came a cat. "Look! Isn't that the same one that attacked Okrim?" The animal stopped near the fire to look at the rabbit.

"Meow."

Maria scratched her head as she studied the large cat. There was something familiar about it. *White paws and chest, orange back . . . Where have I seen a cat like that before? Wait!* "Tristan, look at its tail! See the orange and black bands? See how the black fur shines as if it were painted? That's not a cat. That's a sirnee!"

Chapter 7

Tristan tilted his head, watched the sirnee for a moment, then looked at Maria.

"Sirnees are very rare. One of the things apprentice magicians have to do is learn about plants and animals." Now her voice softened. "I never reached the stage where Eonoway showed me which plants can cure some diseases."

Tristan pointed to the sirnee.

"I did learn about animals, though, and how what people do affects them. Not just overhunting until there are very few left, but also burning forests to clear land and destroying the homes of the animals who live there. Eonoway wanted me to know that it's our responsibility to care for all animals so they won't become extinct. The example she used was the sirnee."

Now it was Maria's turn to stare as the sirnee sat by the fire licking his paw, then wiping it across his face.

He was big, well built and muscular. Maria guessed he weighed more than fifteen pounds. A blaze of white ran along his nose, from its pink tip to the top of his head. His ears and face were orange except for a circle of white starting halfway up his nose and surrounding his entire jaw.

The white continued down his neck and onto his chest. As the white fur inched its way along the sirnee's side, it gradually changed to orange. His back and tail were various shades of that orange.

What marked the cat a "sirnee" were two distinctive features: twin slanted Vs, one on each side of his head, formed by black lines starting at the edges of his eyes and narrowing to points under his ears; and rich black bands of fur that circled his orange tail every few inches.

Maria laughed once. "Do you remember when Lin said his parents told him stories about magic coming from the faery people who were supposed to have lived here long ago? Well, one of the tales Eonoway told me was that sirnees were supposed to have been the elves' pets. She also told me that centuries ago, people hunted sirnees for their fur. Their numbers never increased after that and the few that survive live in places like this, places anyone hardly ever goes. She thought that was the reason there are so few of them. They can't often find each other to mate."

Tristan took Okrim's knife from his belt. He then raised his hands, palms facing up.

"I don't know. Maybe the sirnee was hiding in the tree and Okrim scared him."

Tristan looked at the sirnee and again lifted his hands.

"I don't know why he's here, either. He can't be hungry. This is his home; he can hunt for himself. He's beautiful, isn't he?"

The sirnee finished washing and walked to Maria. He closed his pale yellow eyes, then opened them slowly. Maria watched his dark pupils contract into narrow slits in the bright sunlight. He placed his front paws on her knee and gently began pushing against it. After a minute, he stopped and returned to the fire.

"What was that all about?"

Tristan didn't answer. He just sat, statue-still, watching the sirnee.

"Aroo-eh" said the sirnee; the rabbit was done.

After Tristan gave the first piece to the sirnee, he and Maria ate the rest. When they left, the sirnee came with them.

A few hours later, when an out-of-breath Maria reached the top of a steep slope, Tristan pointed to the west. Two white snow-covered peaks were in front of them.

"That means the valley heading north can't be too far. I hope it's flat. I'm tired of all this climbing." She sat and leaned against the nearest tree. "If this is the easier way, as the innkeeper said, I wonder what the harder way is like."

The sirnee walked over to Maria and curled up in her lap. When Maria began to pet him, he purred loudly. "Don't get too comfortable. We've got to go soon." The sirnee looked up, tilted his head, and jumped off. "That's strange. You'd think he understood what I said. I wonder why he's staying with us? I'm glad he is, though. It's nice having a pet again. I haven't had one since I was a little girl on my father's farm. Do you think we should give him a name?"

Tristan didn't answer. He just readjusted his travel-pack and started off.

When they stopped in the evening, Tristan went looking for their dinner while Maria made camp. She didn't yell at herself too much because the fire started on the third try.

As soon as she was settled next to it, waiting for Tristan, the sirnee curled himself up in her lap.

"You like being scratched, don't you?"

"Aroo-eh." The sirnee looked at her and leaned his cheek into Maria's hand. As he did, his rear stuck up. Maria moved her hand to scratch him over his tail, and the sirnee stretched up with his hind legs, twisting his neck to rub his cheek against her knee. "Brrr. Brrr."

"If you're going to stay with us, I have to give you a name. I can't keep calling you sirnee."

The sirnee settled down, shaping himself into a ball in the hollow of her lap, while Maria thought about a name. "What should it be," she said to herself as she continued to pet him. "What should . . . Jerold. Now how did I think of that? Is that a good name for you? Shall I call you Jerold?"

"Aroo-eh." The newly named Jerold pushed against Maria's lap and stomach. He purred louder.

"I guess that settles it." Tristan's shadow fell over them.

"Up you go, Jerold. We have to get dinner ready."

Tristan looked at the sirnee and back to her.

"I was thinking about naming him and the name just popped into my head. I think he likes it."

Tristan nodded and dropped a plump rabbit next to the fire.

Two days later they were still heading toward the peaks, still climbing up and down steep slopes, and still looking for a valley that headed toward the north. Each time they rounded a curve or topped a hill, Maria searched for it. And each time she didn't see it, she sighed and plodded after Tristan.

That evening, the western sky looked ominous again and Tristan didn't stop to make camp until the night sky was lit by the twin moons. He was looking for a secure place to set up their lean-to. And he found it. Backed up against a cliff wall, Maria saw a circular boulder resembling a huge stone ball. Wedged into a small space between it and the cliff was a fairly good-sized tree. Several feet away, but also near the cliff wall, were two more trees. When Tristan had finished tying the ropes, the lean-to stretched from tree to tree, with the cliff wall at its back and the boulder at its right.

"Do you think it's going to be a bad storm?"

Tristan shrugged his shoulders.

"Well, my protection spell didn't keep Okrim's arrows from almost hitting me. Maybe it will keep the rain away if the wind blows it into the lean-to." She crossed her arms; Tristan stepped toward her but stopped and shook his head as she began to cast the spell and whisper words into the night. Jerold looked at her, too. Then he walked to the back of the lean-to, curled up, and went to sleep.

The storm started sometime in the middle of the night. Maria woke up when the thundering claps shook the cliff side next to her head. But she was so tired she ignored the pounding rain streaming down the outside of the lean-to, ignored the earth-shaking thunder, and, moving closer to the round boulder next to her, went back to sleep. The next time she woke, she thought the world had ended.

Fire seared Maria's left arm; her fingers were being cut away from her body one inch at a time. Her mouth opened and she screamed until her throat was raw. Vaguely, through eyes glazed over with tears and ears filled with the now-hoarse sounds coming from her throat, Maria saw Tristan standing over her, silently trying to move the boulder that had rolled onto her arm. He almost stepped on her head as he planted his feet in the soggy earth and pushed.

"Meow!" Jerold jumped on her chest and ran away.

Tristan paused. He looked down at her once, then put his shoulder, scraped and bleeding, back to the rock. All Maria felt was agonizing pain. She fainted.

Her eyes fluttered and the pain returned. She saw Tristan standing over her with Okrim's large knife in his hand. He looked down at her shoulder just where her arm disappeared under the rock. Maria shook her head. She wanted to say no, but had no strength. Her arm had become numb, and she felt nothing except a dull pounding pain coming from her hand. Even if he managed to cut her arm away from her body, she wouldn't survive. Tristan wasn't a healer; she would bleed to death in minutes.

I told him . . . let . . . me . . . go home. Just before she fainted again, she saw Tristan throw the knife down and lean back into the boulder.

For a second time, Maria opened her eyes. Tristan was there, and standing next to him was a girl and a young boy. The girl said something and the three of them tried to move the rock together.

Suddenly things became dreamlike to Maria. Everything seemed hazy — nothing had a definite shape. Tristan's hands melted into the rock he was still trying to move. The face of a girl with bright green eyes looked down at her, but when she spoke to Tristan, no sounds came from her mouth. The girl pushed Tristan, and Maria thought she saw the girl's hands disappear into his chest. But they didn't really and Tristan moved aside. Now, all Maria saw was the girl.

This can't be real. I must be dreaming. Through half-open eyes, she saw the impossible. The girl's body began to change its shape. Her arms stretched. They became long and brown and turned into massive animal legs. Her chest widened — expanded; her human legs had changed and now equaled the legs her arms had become. The girl's face altered — white horns popped out of her skull; her nose flattened and grew — the eyes, still green, sank back. The girl was now an enormous animal that stepped carefully over her as it lowered its head to the boulder. Maria fainted for the third time.

When something brushed against her face, Maria opened her eyes. *Still . . . dream . . . ing.* She saw the animal's stomach directly over her as a front hoof almost hit her head, pawing the ground. She heard something — a deep trumpet. She felt something — hands reached under her shoulders and pulled. Her body moved; she was free. The pain, which had begun to stop, returned with the suddenness of a striking snake. Maria was able to stay awake just long enough to see the animal disappear into a human shape. *Im . . . pos . . . si . . .*

Finally called away from a dream, Maria heard Jerold meow. Slowly she opened her eyes. The sky was blue; the sun was shining.

"Hello," said a strange voice.

Maria turned her head. Her eyes had trouble focusing. She blinked. *Where am . . . who are . . .* Besides Tristan, there were two other people looking at her. One was a young boy. The other, a girl close to her age. *Why can't I think? What happened to me?* Maria noticed that both of the strangers had green eyes. She had never seen anyone with green eyes before. *Where have I seen green like that?* Then she took a deep breath and a tinge of pain inched along her arm. *The rock . . . Tristan . . . the girl who turned . . . what is she!*

Maria remembered and became afraid. *What kind of magic does that girl have? Is it dark magic? Even Eonoway can't do that.* Maria scrambled back, but Tristan quickly moved behind her, putting his hands under her shoulders and helping her to a sitting position.

"What . . . What are you? How did you do that?" The girl just stood there, watching her, not saying anything. "Who are you?" said Maria, not quite shouting, but speaking louder than normal.

"I'm someone who helped you," answered the girl.

Helped me! What dark magic have you helped me with? "How?" stammered Maria. "How did you do it? No one can do what you did! Not even a sorceress, and the last sorceress died a thousand years ago. What magic do you know? What kind of magic is it?" But the girl remained silent. "I have to know," said Maria, raising her voice, "What kind of magic is it?"

"I'm not a sorceress," answered the girl. "I'm just someone who was here when you needed help."

"People don't change into animals! They can't." Maria began to stand and leaned on Tristan for support. When she got to her feet, her arm brushed against Tristan's leg. She studied her hand carefully. *It's whole! My hand and arm are whole!* "Sorceresses do this," she whispered.

71

"I didn't do that," answered the girl.

"How can you say that? My hand was crushed, I felt it. Not even a Magician of the First Order could heal it. What kind of magic did you use?" said Maria, moving her fingers. "Was it dark magic?"

"I don't know how to do magic," answered the girl.

"What do you call . . . that?" Maria pointed to the boulder she had been trapped under. "Of course it's magic." Next, Maria raised her healed hand to the level of the girl's face. "What do you call this? I asked you what kind of magic you used. Why won't you tell me? Was it dark magic?"

"I told you," said the girl, "I didn't fix your hand."

"He did," said the boy, pointing to Tristan.

"No," answered Maria. "He couldn't have. He can't speak. That's impossible."

"He d–did. And the cat helped, too," repeated the boy.

"The sirnee?" Maria turned and looked at Jerold lying on a rock warming himself in the sun. "He's just a cat."

"But they did it," insisted the boy.

"Is that true?" said Maria, turning to look at Tristan. He reminded her of the first time she had seen him — dirty face, torn clothes, black eyes staring deep into hers. *How could that be? Even Eonoway couldn't make the magic do the simplest things unless she said the words. She told me thinking them wasn't enough. How could he do magic like this without speaking? This was no simple spell. Eonoway couldn't be SO wrong.*

He just looked at her with the same stare he always used. "Tristan, is it true!" When he didn't answer, when he didn't nod or lift his arms, Maria took a small step toward him, closing both of her hands into fists. "I asked you if you did this!" His head slowly moved up and down; Maria backed away. "How could you do that! How can you use the magic without saying the words? You didn't just start a fire, you used magic — powerful magic. You have to say the words and you can't speak!"

Tristan did nothing. Maria became so angry she found it hard to breath. "Why are you letting me stay with you? You don't need me. I'll never be a magician. I can't do anything right. I couldn't make the spell to keep us safe work, and I said the words right. I did! All I am is a tagalong. I'm going to get you killed if I stay with you. Do you understand that!"

Maria felt tears form in her eyes and found it hard to say her next sentence. "I want to go back to Deventap." She thought her calming spell and found breathing easier. She gently whispered as she sat down. "Go on without me, Tristan. I can't help you."

Tristan shook his head. Then he walked to the fire and picked up a piece of freshly cooked meat. That's when Maria noticed someone had caught an animal. She looked around as Tristan came back toward her and saw a large wolf. But before she had time to wonder where the wolf had come from, Tristan handed her the meat. Maria realized how hungry she was. She took it, closed her eyes, and took a deep breath. It smelled good; she thought her calming spell once more just to stop herself from forcing the entire strip into her mouth at one time.

"I'm . . . I'm sorry," she said to Tristan. "You saved my life and I yelled at you. I shouldn't have done that." He walked back to the fire.

Now Maria looked up into the faces of the other two who stood near her. *What do I say to them? What do I say to someone who can* . . . "I don't know who you are . . . I don't know what you are, but you saved my life, too. Thank you."

"My name's Susan, this is Jeffrey, and that's Farrun," answered Susan, looking at the wolf. "If you'd like to thank me, then promise never to tell anyone what happened, what you saw, what I did."

Strange, she has such a soft voice for so powerful a magician. And she's so young. Maria finished the meat in her hand. *I'm just as old as she is and yet she has so much more . . . Why did I ever think I could be a magician?*

"Wha–what's a Magician of the First Order?" asked Jeffrey.

"You're not from Kestra, are you?"

"No," answered Susan. "We come from Reune."

"My name's Maria. This is Tristan. I call the sirnee Jerold." Maria's stomach growled, and she knew she had to eat more. She got up and walked to the fire. Tristan pointed to a soup simmering in their pot next to the flames, and she began to sip it from her spoon. She looked at the girl who had joined her at the fire. *Where did she get the power to change her shape? Eonoway never even mentioned a magic like that. I wish I could do it.* "What are you?" Maria finally said. "What magic do you use? I've never heard of anyone doing what you did."

"And I never heard of anyone doing what he did," said Susan, looking at Tristan.

Maria didn't answer. She couldn't. *What can I say? Even Befany doesn't understand how Tristan does magic, and if I knew, I still couldn't tell Susan anything. Eonoway warned me the last time we met that if I ever told anyone outside the Order of Magicians what I know about magic, then any magician, even a lesser one, has the right to kill me. I know she saved my life but I can't tell her about the magic.*

The silence dragged on, broken only by the sounds of the fire's crackle and people eating. Tristan finally broke it by snapping a stick to get their attention; then after looking from Susan to her, he tapped his ear — then his lips.

"I think he means that we each have our secrets," said Maria.

Again, the only thing Maria heard was the popping fire. She watched Susan shift her body as if the ground had suddenly become too hard to sit on. *If I could learn her power, if I could shape change like that, Eonoway would have to take me back.* But as soon as Maria thought about her former teacher, she stopped herself. *Who am I fooling? Even if Susan did tell me how she does it, I'd never be able to do it.*

"It's all right," Maria said. "You don't have to say anything if you don't want to. I may not be a very good magician, but I know that magicians guard their magic. I won't ask you again. You did enough."

The girl with green eyes smiled.

"What did Tristan do?" asked Jeffrey. "Can anyone learn to do it? Could I?"

"I don't know what he did. I really don't. You see, Tristan . . ." Maria lifted the bowl to her mouth and swallowed the last of the soup. Then she listened to the fire and watched the flames. "I can't tell you, Jeffrey. I'm sorry, but I can't."

75

Susan and Jeffrey said nothing more as they finished their meal. When both of them were done, Susan got up. "We have to leave. Our clan is in danger, and we're going home to help."

"Things aren't going well in Kestra, either," answered Maria. "That's why we're here. The king of Yunii wants to rule the four nations and has attacked us. We're going to Yunii and try to steal some of their magic."

"I hope you find what you're looking for," said Susan.

Maria reached for Susan's hand. "I don't understand who you are or what you can do. But I promise we'll never tell anyone what happened. I just wish there was something more I could do to repay you."

Susan smiled as she stared into Maria's eyes. "Keeping my secret is enough."

Maria took one step back. "Jeffrey, I can't tell you what you wanted to know. But there's someone else who might. Her name is Befany. She lives in Deventap and when we get home, we'll be staying with her. I can't promise, but if everything works out for you and your clan, come to see us. I'll ask Befany to tell you."

"Befany," answered Susan. "I'll remember her name. Thank you, Maria. Come on, Farrun, let's go."

Maria sat on the ground staring at the curve in the path where Susan, Jeffrey, and the wolf had disappeared. When Tristan gave her another meat strip, she looked up at him. "How *can* you do magic, Tristan?" she quietly asked.

Tristan usually never answered questions like this and Maria knew it. So she was surprised when he kneeled down next to her and drew a small rectangle with a hole in it. He pointed to the hole and then to himself. Next, he pointed back at the hole and then to her.

"You found your own way, didn't you?" she asked.

He nodded.

"But . . ."

He stopped her by placing a finger across her mouth. Then he pointed down as he stood.

"I have to find my own way, too," she said as he turned and went back to the fire.

Jerold startled her when he appeared and curled up in her lap. Maria petted him and he purred loudly. "And how did you help?" she whispered. "I'll bet you just wanted to stay near me. You might be smart, but you're not magic. Animals can't do magic."

"Burr. Burr." Jerold twisted on his back and let his paws dangle. When Maria began to scratch him under the chin, he wrapped his front legs around her wrist. He carefully put his teeth around her thumb and gently bit her as he kicked out with his rear legs. Maria laughed as she rubbed his stomach with her other hand. After a moment of that, Jerold stopped, tucked his head under his hind legs, and went to sleep.

Feeling the sun's warmth, listening to Tristan opening their packs and putting their things out to dry, Maria relaxed and began to think. She turned when Tristan tore the cowhide that was still under the boulder. There would be no more lean-tos. *Eonoway WAS wrong! She told me that the spells had to be recited the way they always had or else they wouldn't work.* All of a sudden something Lin said came into her mind and for the first time, Maria really understood what he meant. *Eonoway wanted me to wear shoes that won't fit my feet. What did Eonoway say when she told me to leave? I had innate power, more native ability than anyone she had ever taught. Can I learn on my own? Can I do without help what Eonoway couldn't teach me in three years of apprenticing?*

Jerold moved, twisting his neck and pushing against her with his head.

I don't know, Jerold, she thought as she continued rubbing his stomach.

"Murr."

Chapter 8

The next morning, after three hours of walking, Tristan pointed down a steep hill, and Maria saw a long wide valley heading north. It took a while to reach it, but once they did, they realized that the innkeeper had given them good advice. As far as they could see, the land was flat. After resting for a short time, they started toward Yunii.

Jerold stayed. Sometimes he walked near them; sometimes he ran ahead and disappeared for hours. But he usually returned after dark and nestled himself in whoever's lap was closest to the fire. Maria offered him scraps of dried meat, but usually Jerold just sniffed them. Obviously, he hunted for himself. Maria wished hunting for them was as easy. But whatever animals lived in the valley saw the two of them coming long before Tristan's sling could knock them down. After four days, they had run out of supplies. They made camp early that fourth evening and just as Tristan was about to leave for the mountain slopes to hunt for dinner, Maria saw Jerold, who had run off an hour earlier. The sirnee was coming toward them with a large bird clamped tightly in his mouth. He dropped it by the fire. This was the first time he had hunted for them.

"How did you know we were out of food? You know, Tristan, I may be crazy but I don't think sirnees are just large cats. Do you?"

"Aroo-eh."

Tristan signed no answer as he picked up the bird and began preparing it.

Five days and one thunderstorm later, they reached the valley's end. Again, just as the innkeeper had said, Maria saw several trails, each veering eastward through the mountains. "Which one?" she asked. "They all lead to Yunii."

Tristan shrugged his shoulders and started down the closest path.

"Meow!" Jerold ran a few steps and rubbed his cheek against Tristan's leg. Then he trotted up a small steep hill.

"I think he wants us to go that way." Tristan began to raise his hands but she shook her head. "I don't know. But I don't know why Jerold stayed with us or how he knew we needed food in the valley, either. He wants us to go that way. Since we don't know where any of these trails lead, we might as well take the one he wants."

Tristan nodded and helped Maria climb the sharp slope. When they reached the top, Jerold walked away. Every few yards, the sirnee turned his head slightly to make sure they were following. For the next four days Jerold walked in front of them, leading them where he wanted, closer and closer to the border of Yunii.

"Why are you taking us this way?" Maria asked Jerold

that night as he lay in her lap. "How do you know where we want to go?" Jerold sleepily stared into her eyes, mrrred once, and put his head back down. "If you could only talk to me," said Maria, scratching him under the chin. "Wouldn't it be great if there were a magic spell I could say that would let us talk to each other? But that's impossible, isn't it?" Jerold didn't answer. He just stretched his neck so Maria could give him good, long scratches and went to sleep.

The next morning they came to a large stream rushing down the mountainside. Jerold followed it northeast. Other streams, filled with the runoff from the mountain storms, joined it, and as they descended, they were soon following a swollen river. In a few days, the land opened, the mountains became rolling hills, and Maria realized that they were almost in Yunii.

When the last hill had disappeared, Maria and Tristan looked across the river at huge trees growing on the other side. Tristan sat, pulling Maria down with him, and drew the bone shape outline of the four nations in the ground. He drew a triangular-shaped wedge in southern Yunii, starting at the edge of the mountains. Then he sketched two wavy lines on both sides of the wedge, and where the lines met at the top, he added one more line heading north.

"You know where we are, don't you?"

He nodded his head.

Jerold sat in her lap. Maria petted him; he purred. "I don't know any landmarks in Yunii. What's that?" she asked, pointing to the forest on the other side of the river.

Tristan touched the center of the triangle.

"The forest is that wedge and this river's one of the wavy lines."

Again, Tristan nodded.

"That means we're here," she said, putting a finger on his map where the Thundrous Mountains ended and the forested land in front of them began.

For the third time, Tristan nodded.

Just then, Jerold got up. "Meeeooww!" The sound was long and drawn out, and Maria was so startled she thought something was wrong. She quickly rose and stepped toward the sirnee, but Jerold ran to the edge of the water. He faced the huge trees and cried again. "Meeeooww. Meeeooww!"

"Do you think he wants us to cross the river?"

Suddenly Jerold hissed, arching his back and raising the fur along his neck.

Tristan shook his head.

"I think you're right. Don't worry, Jerold, we won't cross the river. I just wish you'd tell me how you always seem to understand what we say." Maria looked down at the map and then back to Jerold. "If the wedge is that forest, we don't want to go there. We have to go east, farther into Yunii."

"Rowl."

"Well," Maria said to Tristan, "we're in Yunii. Where do you want to go now?"

Tristan made two fists and held his hands up. He moved his head from left to right as if reading a scroll.

"The magician's library. Befany said that was in Casgarn."

Tristan nodded, got up, and started.

For the first few days, traveling through large patches of woods that were too small to be called forests and over ground too rocky to be farmed, they saw no one. Jerold stayed with them but he no longer hunted. Tristan's flying rocks hit enough small animals and birds to keep all three fed.

On the third day, the land changed. The rocky ground gave way to topsoil rich enough to support farms. It was high summer now, and they saw people in the distance working in the long, flat fields. Late in the afternoon, they stopped next to a small sign.

"Felena," Maria read.

Tristan took off his travel-pack and rummaged through it. He pulled out a small pouch filled with Yuniian coins, some given to them by Befany, and some taken from the soldiers who had attacked Lin's cottage. He put the pouch into his pocket.

"Before we go, what do I say when people ask me where we're from?"

Tristan thought a moment. Then, he wrote the word *Maceron* on the ground.

"What's that?"

He drew the four nations again and pointed to the top of Yunii, almost next to the Azure Lake, a large lake that touched a major portion of Yunii's northern border. Then he pointed to the sign saying Felena and back to Maceron.

"Maceron is a town, right?" Tristan nodded. Soon, the green of the fields disappeared and yellow-brown grass took its place. The road they followed became dry and dusty. After half an hour, they saw the small village of Felena. From where they stood, they could see the first and last house on the main street. There couldn't have been more than a couple of dozen buildings.

"Meow."

Maria stopped. It took her a moment to locate Jerold. Usually, he walked in front, but when she looked, he was gone.

"Meow."

Jerold was eight or nine feet behind.

"We have to go into town. We need supplies, and I'd like a bath. You can stay with us. We won't let anyone bother you."

Jerold looked at her, then turned and ran away.

"Jerold! Jerold!" But the sirnee disappeared into the grass. "Tristan, why did he do that? How are we going to find him when we leave Felena?"

Tristan shrugged his shoulders. As they walked past the first building, Maria stopped and spoke to an elderly man sitting on a porch with a broken railing and patches of wood missing from its roof. "Is there an inn here?"

The man leaned forward. "Halfway down, on the other side of the road. Are you planning to stay long?" Before Maria could answer, the man continued speaking. "If you are, I've got some small jobs for your young man, if he wants the work. Ever since the war started, most of the young men have been taken by the reds."

"Reds?" asked Maria.

"Helborat's magician-lords. I just call them reds for short. How come he's not in the army?"

Maria looked at Tristan who was standing next to her brushing the dirt off his pants. "My brother can't talk,"

84

she said, deciding that calling him brother was the easiest way of explaining why they were together.

The man rubbed his chin as he stared at Tristan. "He might be the lucky one if the war doesn't go the way the reds said it would. Anyway, the offer's still good if you stay."

Maria thanked him and went to the inn. The inside was dark, even though the shutters on the two windows were still open. The sun was low, the night lanterns had not been lit, and except for a young girl who was scrubbing the tops of the long wooden tables with a wet rag, the common room was empty.

"We'd like a room," said Maria.

The girl stopped working. Maria thought she couldn't have been older than ten or eleven. The girl dropped the rag into a bucket and wiped her hands on a dirty smock. "I'll get my master."

"Master?" whispered Maria.

The girl reappeared, followed by an innkeeper with a large potbelly. "Get on with your work." The innkeeper walked to Maria, but before he spoke, he turned his head and faced the little worker. "I want those tables cleaned before you help the cook. The evening crowd will be here soon." The girl quickly ran back to the bucket and continued washing the table tops. "So, you want a room?"

"Yes. We'd like a couple of baths and a hot meal, too."

The innkeeper looked at Maria carefully, moving his head slowly up and down. Then he did the same for Tristan. "How long are you planning to stay?"

"Not very long. We're going to Casgarn."

"Don't know why you want to go there. That place is

filling up with refugees from the north faster than I can fill a pail from the well."

From the north? Kestra is south. What's happening in Yunii that's causing refugees? When Maria began listening again to the innkeeper, she had missed the first part of his next sentence.

". . . doesn't like it, either. Too many people are cluttering up the capital's street. Where are you from?"

"Maceron."

"Rumor says the fighting has been pretty bad up that way. What happened?"

Not knowing what the man was talking about, Maria was glad when Tristan answered. He knelt down, pretending to warm his hands over a fire. Then his fingers moved rapidly as he stood up and spread out his arms.

"What's the matter with him?" the man asked.

"He can't talk," answered Maria.

"That explains why he's still with you," said the man more to himself than to her. "So, you were burned out. If you're going to Casgarn, how come you're here? You passed the main road to Casgarn. The city is northeast of Felena."

Tristan looked at Maria, and she knew she'd have to answer the innkeeper. But she was never a good liar. "We . . . we had an uncle who lived . . . near the river west of here. We tried to find him but couldn't."

"What's the man's name? Maybe I know him."

"Linster." Maria used the only name she could think of quickly.

The innkeeper shook his head. "Never heard of him. Since you couldn't find him, how about staying here? I could use some help in the inn. There's work for both of you. What do you say?"

Maria shook her head. "No, thank you. We have family in Casgarn."

"Suit yourself," the innkeeper answered. "Room and two meals, three coppers each a day. Bath's an extra two. You have to pay in advance."

Tristan took out his pouch and counted out six coins. He put them in his palm and held them out. But when the innkeeper reached out, Tristan pulled his hand away. He closed his fist and pretended to scrub his arm. Then pointing to Maria, he picked up an imaginary bucket and emptied the water. After that, he opened his palm again.

The innkeeper looked at the coins and then back to Tristan. "All right. Six coppers and one bath apiece. Agreed?"

Tristan handed him the money.

"Girl! Show them to room three. When you want your baths, tell her. The bathing room is next to the kitchen. She'll heat the water and tell you when the tub's full." Maria nodded as she followed their guide up the stairs.

Remembering their last dinner in an inn, the two decided to eat early. The common room held only a few customers and they showed no interest in the strangers. After working long hours in the fields, the men were only interested in complaining to each other. Maria and Tristan listened carefully.

"Blasted war," said one farmer. "With my son recently drafted into service, I've had to do the work for both of us."

"At least he's still alive, Kelnor," answered another.

"The magician–lords took my son several months ago and sent him up north to fight against Prince Chan. The fighting's been bad there, and I don't know if he's alive or dead."

"It's not natural," said a third man, "a son trying to kill his father. Chan should have waited until the king died. He will, eventually. Then the prince would have been king without a rebellion."

Kelnor looked around, and his eyes stopped when they saw Maria and Tristan. He lowered his voice but the two heard anyway. "Listen, James, you know why the prince did it. This war won't stop even if Kestra surrenders. It won't stop until Helborat is emperor of the four nations. A lot of our sons are going to die. Chan just wanted to stop it."

"He isn't doing very well," answered James. "As a matter of fact, he's making life harder on those of us who are staying behind. The produce we have to deliver to the king's garrison has been increased. There's more men in the army and it's farmers like us who have to feed them."

"And don't forget the money Helborat needs to fight this war, Kelnor," said the second man. "Who do you think will pay for the horses and weapons the army needs? I know the prince meant well, but he didn't think it out. When he didn't kill his father, he made everyone in Yunii suffer more. If he really wanted to help us, as he says, he'd give himself up."

Kelnor didn't answer. He just drained whatever was in his mug and asked the innkeeper to fill it up again.

"So that's what's happening," whispered Maria. "Yunii is not only fighting us, they're fighting themselves. I wonder if Prince Chan is winning? But even if he isn't, the civil war might help us. If we can find some of the refugees the innkeeper told us about, we could blend in. We would be just two more people heading for Casgarn."

Tristan stopped eating long enough to nod. After finishing their meal, the two would have liked to bathe, but when they saw the young girl wearily serving the people drinks and food, they decided not to ask. Instead, they went to their room and fell asleep almost immediately.

They took their baths the next day after breakfast and, feeling refreshed, decided to leave Felena. On the way out, they passed a small shop that served as a bakery and general store. Parting with four more coins, the travelers walked away with several days' rations. As they left the village, Maria kept looking over her shoulder.

"Where's Jerold? He knows where we're going, I'm sure of it. Why didn't he just wait for us on this side of the village?" Tristan didn't answer.

By late morning, the northern path they followed had taken them through several small woods and farm fields. As in Kestra, it seemed the villages of Yunii were built on land not suitable for farms. Then the land abruptly became hilly, with large boulders sticking up haphazardly everywhere. Maria kept turning around hoping to see the black-and-orange sirnee. But each time she did, Tristan gently tugged at her arm. In midafternoon, the twisting road they followed entered a forest, the first real forest they had encountered since leaving the river near the Thundrous Mountains. Tristan decided to camp for the night.

As the pair sat by a small fire, they heard it. "Aroo-eh,

aroo-eh." Coming toward them between the trees was Jerold. Maria ran, picked him up, and squashed him. Jerold put up with it for a moment before wriggling out of her arms to settle on one of the packs near the fire.

"You found us!"

"Murr. Murr." Jerold stretched. His legs pushed out, his head moved back, and his pink tongue stuck out just a little. But the pack was not wide enough and the sirnee abruptly fell off. Tristan smiled; Maria laughed.

"Rowl!" Jerold looked at the two, then jumped back on the pack and curled up into a ball with his back to the fire.

Two days later, the three left the forest; but it took several more days to reach the road to Casgarn. That road headed east and was cluttered with northern refugees who had lost their homes and farms in the civil war. Tristan and Maria joined them.

"Did you notice something?" asked Maria when the two of them broke out of the slow-moving line to eat lunch. "There are very few young people. Look at that!" She pointed to an elderly man and woman pulling a two-wheeled cart stuffed with their belongings. "The people we're seeing are either like that or young children. Where are the young men and women? They can't all be in the army, can they?"

Jerold, who had stayed with them even after the two had joined the line of refugees, suddenly meowed. Riding toward them was a company of soldiers, and leading them was a man in the bright red robe of a full Yuniian magician.

Chapter 9

It was probably just unlucky that the magician happened to be on Maria and Tristan's side of the road, but knowing that didn't make Maria feel any better. She swallowed the dry bread in her mouth, quickly recited her calming spell, and held Tristan's hand. Both stood when the magician-lord raised his hand to halt the soldiers.

Maria looked up. Even in the daylight, it was impossible to see the magician-lord's face. A hood was pulled over his head with the bottom tied closed to keep out sand and dust. When the magician spoke, his voice sounded a bit muffled, but Maria recognized the tone immediately. It was the same tone Eonoway had used when she was angry and wanted no backtalk from whomever she was angry with.

"Where are you going, girl?" said the voice.

"Casgarn."

"Where are you from?"

"Maceron."

"Have you people from the north, who run and hide at the first sign of trouble instead of staying to defend

91

your king, forgotten how to address those of my order?"

What is he . . . At that moment a little girl walking by started crying, obviously afraid of the magician, and Maria was reminded of the serving girl at the inn.

"I'm sorry, Master," she said. "We are from Maceron."

"That's better." He turned to Tristan. "Who are you?"

"He is my brother, Master," answered Maria.

The magician–lord moved his horse a bit closer to Maria, forcing her back. "I asked him, girl."

"He can't talk. That is why he was allowed to stay with me and not join the army."

"Look at me, boy!" said the voice within the hood. When Tristan looked up, the magician raised one hand and whispered into the air.

"Eewow gerinta sinkrata discot.

"What say you, boy?"

The truth spell! The same one we use in Kestra!

Tristan said nothing.

The red hood nodded and turned back to Maria. "Why are you going to Casgarn?"

"We have family there, Master."

"I asked you *why* you were going?"

"I'm sorry, Master," said Maria. "Our home was destroyed in the fighting."

"Where are your parents?"

"Dead, Master."

Again the hood nodded. "Listen to me, girl. Too many people are fleeing to Casgarn. There is not enough food to feed them or places for them to sleep. The city's dirty enough without more people crowding in, especially those with cats."

Jerold, who was sitting next to Maria, looked up but made no sound.

"A tent city has sprung up on the outside of the city's walls and the king doesn't like it. Anyone who doesn't live in Casgarn now will not be allowed in the city."

Why is he telling us this? What does he want? "Thank you for telling us, Master. If we cannot go to Casgarn, what do you suggest?"

The magician untied the hood's cord and with a shake of his head, tossed the hood back, giving Maria a clear view of his face.

He was a youngish man, maybe in his late thirties, with long brown hair that reached the edge of his shoulders. His face was clean shaven, but his cheeks were covered with pockmarks. As he looked down at Maria and Tristan, he never lowered his head, just his eyes. "I suggest you turn north at the next crossroads and go to Caberta. It should take you about two weeks." He reached into his pocket and pulled out a small silver token. "This is my mark," he said, tossing it to Maria. "Go to my manor." He stretched, lifting his body a few inches off the saddle. When he was settled again, he continued. "The large estates are short handed and mine is no exception. There is work for you both in Caberta. You will be fed, clothed, and housed in safety."

"Thank you, Master."

The magician-lord nodded. "Tell my overseer to train you for work in the house. Your brother will work where the overseer needs him the most."

"Yes, Master. Thank you."

"You are now in my employ. You will refer to me as Lord Jerbin or my Lord."

"Yes, my Lord."

"I will ask your names when I return home. Tell the overseer that should be before the harvest." Lord Jerbin did not wait for an answer. He pulled his hood back over his head, tied it, and rode off.

Maria looked at the coin in her palm. It was polished silver and stamped on it was the name "Jerbin." Tristan looked, too, and then smiled.

"What's that for?"

He held his hands up and pretended to read. Then he took Maria's hands and made them into a tentlike shape, her thumb and pinky at the edges and the three middle fingers making the peak.

"The library in Casgarn?"

Tristan nodded as he held Jerbin's coin and moved it under her fingers.

"You think Jerbin's mark will get us into the magician's library?"

Tristan continued smiling.

"Aroo-eh."

"I hope you're both right," she said, as the three rejoined the steadily moving line of refugees. "Maybe Jerbin's mark will get us into the city, too." Thirteen days later, just as the morning sun was getting hot, it did.

As they approached the city, the line ground to a halt while soldiers stopped and questioned everyone. When it was Maria's turn, all she did was show the mark and say they were on an errand for their master. The coin opened the way.

The first thing that impressed Maria about Casgarn was the huge wall surrounding it. The bottom half was made of square blocks of stone neatly stacked on top of each other. The top half was upright logs, each tied securely to those next to it. All Maria could see of the city as she neared the drawbridge were the tops of the tallest towers. In front of the wall, just as Jerbin had said, Maria saw hundreds of tents and wagons.

Maria had never been to any large city and her first view of this one was shocking. The houses near the drawbridge were nothing more than huts packed tightly together, and a ditch with foul-smelling stagnant water ran in front of them. The people she saw were poorly clothed and went about their business with blank stares on their faces. No one looked at Maria or Tristan as they walked through the crowded streets.

"Where should we go?" she whispered.

Tristan pointed to a tower at the back of the city and followed the dirt road that led to it. Jerold, who was still with them, walked between the two. Children sitting along the edge of the ditch pointed, oohing and ahhing at the "pretty cat." The adults, however, paid no attention. No one in Casgarn remembered what a sirnee was and thought Jerold was just a large cat.

The road ended and the three stood before a grassy field dotted with grazing horses. At the far end was another wall, similar to the outside one only much smaller. A large metal gate was in the center.

At the gate, Maria showed Jerbin's coin and spoke to the guards through the metal bars. "My lord Jerbin has sent us to the library. This is our first time here and we don't know where to go."

"Which library?" asked a soldier, looking at the coin.

Which library? How . . . "I don't understand."

"There's the library in the palace," said the guard, who went back to eating some bread and cheese. "The magicians use that for histories. Then there's the one in the temple. But no one except magician–lords are allowed there."

"That's the one I have to go to," said Maria. "My master needs the wording of a spell. He . . ."

"Don't explain it to me, girl," snapped the guard. "*I* don't care. Tell it to whoever opens the temple door. Follow the main road past the palace. The temple is straight ahead." He waited to finish his last bite before opening the door to let Maria and Tristan in.

"Hey! What's that cat doing? We've got enough cats in the compound."

Tristan held Maria's hand tightly and sped up.

"Didn't you hear . . ." The guard didn't leave his post to follow.

Now this is how a capital should look. It was as if they had entered a different city. The large houses were made of wood or stone. Gardens of grass, small trees, bushes, and flowers grew in front of them. Even the streets were not the same. Instead of dirt paths, hundreds of flat rocks were set into the earth, paving the roads.

"I wouldn't mind living here," she whispered to Tristan.

"Meow!"

It took about twenty minutes of brisk walking before they reached the palace, a long, two-level structure with soldiers standing at intervals along a low wall surrounding it. Since Maria and Tristan did not attempt to enter the palace grounds, the guards ignored them. They turned a corner, followed the road toward the back of the palace, and saw a huge stone building with two columns, each at least thirty feet high, holding up a porch roof. The door was open and no guards were in front. Maria stopped and raised a hand over her eyes but she couldn't see into the building. The doorway loomed in front of them like a giant mouth waiting for its next meal.

"Rowl."

"I wish I knew what Jerold means. What do you want to do, go in now or wait until dark?" She watched Tristan as he stared at the open door.

"Rowl!"

Tristan took a deep breath, gently touched her hand, and headed straight ahead. The midmorning air was hot, but once they passed through the entrance, it became cool, almost chilly. Facing them was a closed door. Tristan held up an imaginary scroll. Next, he drew a long rectangle in the air, and finally, pointed at the door.

"I don't understand."

Tristan's eyes half closed.

"Well, I'm sorry, but I don't."

He kneeled down and pretended to push something. Then stood, brushing invisible dirt from his pants and her dress. Tracing the rectangle again, he pointed out the doorway, toward the south.

97

"You mean when we pushed Lin? Is that the rectangle you drew, Lin's glass coffin?"

He nodded, then held up Jerbin's mark.

"I think I know! You want me to say Lord Jerbin wants the counterspell to the magic that created the glass coffin. Right?"

Tristan smiled. They knocked, and in a few minutes, the door was opened by a man wearing a pale pink robe. The room beyond was brightly lit, making it hard for Maria to see the young man's face clearly. However, there was no mistaking the sound of disgust in his voice when he demanded to know what business the two of them had.

Maria took the coin from Tristan's hand and held it high. When the man spoke again, the harshness in his voice disappeared.

"I am Tasinlo, apprentice to Lord Re-in. How may I serve Lord Jerbin?"

An apprentice! What luck! Instantly, Maria remembered her own apprenticeship and how, whenever some visitor to Eonoway's castle gazed at her with respect, she felt as if she were the magician she always dreamed of becoming. *Though this apprentice is older than I am, if I can make him feel really important, he might get the counterspell for us.*

She bowed low. "My master, Lord Jerbin, asked me to seek you out." Instantly, Tasinlo stood tall and licked his fingers before running his hands over his hair. "My master has heard how well you are performing and wonders if you would grant him a favor. He is busy and cannot return to the library himself."

98

"Lord Jerbin asks a favor from me?" Tasinlo's chest puffed out.

"Yes, Master," answered Maria, bowing again. "My lord bade me to say that you, Tasinlo, can be trusted with his delicate request."

Tasinlo smiled broadly. "Lord Jerbin." He nodded slowly and stepped back. "Is *that* with you?" he said, looking at Jerold.

"Yes, Master."

Tasinlo shook his head but did not close the door until all three were inside. Maria turned to speak but the apprentice was already walking down the hallway. At the end was a staircase, and Tasinlo, with his head high and back stiff, went down. He turned left at the bottom, passing three closed doors, then stopped to open a fourth.

Maria recognized the room. It was just like the one she had had in Eonoway's tower, a small apprentice's cell, holding only a bed, desk, and chair.

"How may I serve the great Lord Jerbin?"

Maria's stomach churned and her heart seemed to beat loudly; seeing the room brought back memories, memories of dreams she once had. This man, filled with praise, might have the same dreams. If he did, she could trick him. *If I convince Tasinlo to find the counterspell, then Befany would have been right to send me with Tristan. I wouldn't have been just a tagalong.* She swallowed noisily before speaking. *I'll tell him mostly truth. It will sound better that way.* "My lord bids me to tell you this. There is a man imprisoned in a glasslike box. My master wishes to free that person but does not know the counterspell. He cannot ask other magician–lords for he doesn't know who cast the spell. Lord Jerbin begs you to search the scrolls for the counterspell and show it to my brother."

"Does this have anything to do with the key the masters are searching for?" whispered Tasinlo.

Maria, confused, simply nodded and bowed.

"Does Lord Jerbin think he may be close to finding it?"

Again, Maria just bowed.

Tasinlo sat on the chair. He ran his hands over his hair and then absentmindedly arranged several loose papers on his desk into a neat pile. "Lord Jerbin is one of the eight great lords. If he found it, he could become kin . . ." He stopped suddenly, shot to his feet, and spun around to face Maria. His next words came rapidly. "Why does the great lord ask for me?"

"I have told you. My lord has heard of the work you do. If he could . . ." *What was the name of Tasinlo's master? Think, Maria, what was the name?*

Re-in.

The name floated into her mind, and Maria rattled on. "He would ask Lord Re-in for you, but he cannot offend your lord."

Tasinlo nodded. "Who would have guessed?" he whispered to himself. "Jerbin *is* right, of course. He cannot offend Re-in because the old man has the king's ear. Re-in's cries of my not learning fast enough are not true. As I suspected, he is afraid I learn too much, too quickly. But if Jerbin finds the key and . . ."

"My lord bids me to say that if you can help him in this matter, if you could find the counterspell, he will never

100

forget your kindness. He will always remember your name in both word and deed."

Tasinlo noisily sucked in his next breath; his cheeks turned red as he rubbed his chin. After being silent for a long while, a smile crossed his lips. He stood tall again and nodded. "Ever since a scroll was stolen from us many years ago, it is forbidden to show them to one who is not a magician. If I discover the spell, I will have to bring it to Lord Jerbin myself."

"This . . . this must be kept secret. Lord Jerbin cannot be seen with you. Though my brother cannot speak, he can write. I . . . I will not be present when you show him the scroll. He will remember and write it for my lord. That is why Lord Jerbin chose us. No one must ever know."

Tasinlo sat quietly on the edge of the bed. Obviously, he was in a dilemma. "I would like to do what Lord Jerbin commands. But if I do, I may have to look at the sacred scrolls. Apprentices cannot do that unless a lord is present. If I was caught, I could be killed."

"Are there any lords in the temple who might see you?"

Tasinlo quickly stood up and began pacing again. "No. None of the lords is staying here now. They are all in their palace quarters and will remain until the king leaves. Besides the two of you, who knows of Lord Jerbin's request?"

"I have told you. Only the four of us."

"Did he write anything to me so I may know you speak the truth?"

"No, Master. It would be too dangerous. We have lived in Caberta all our lives, and of all his servants, my Lord Jerbin trusts us most. He places that trust in you as well, knowing that you will forget his request once we leave."

Tasinlo smiled. "You will stay here while I see what can be done." As he turned, he noticed Jerold curled up in the corner. "Do not let it on the bed."

Both Maria and Tristan bowed low to him. "Yes, Master." Tasinlo blushed slightly again as he left.

Chapter 10

As soon as Tasinlo left, Jerold jumped onto the bed. Now, the three waited . . . and waited. It wasn't easy, but they had no choice. They couldn't leave even if they had wanted to. Maria said nothing and spent most of her time sitting, petting Jerold. Hearing him purr and brushing his fur over and over soothed her almost as well as the calming spell. Time dragged on. The small slit in the top of the wall that passed for a window didn't give enough light for Maria to know how late it was becoming.

Eventually, she and Tristan became hungry and ate sparingly from their dwindling supplies. Finally, the door opened and Tasinlo appeared. His face was pale; his breathing rapid. Jerold jumped down but the apprentice didn't notice. He remained with his back against the door, eyes closed, and a small bundle clutched in his arms. Maria saw his lips move; his breathing slowed. After a moment, he spoke.

"Tell Lord Jerbin that I looked in most of the common scrolls and found nothing. Make sure you say that I, Tasinlo, because the great lord wished it, not only went into the holy room, but actually took the three sacred scrolls. I will start reading them now. However they must be returned before morning's light. If they are not, they will be discovered missing. Luck was with us, for tonight it was my turn to inspect the holy room to see that the scrolls are safe."

When Tasinlo turned around to put the scrolls on his desk, Tristan hit him on the back of his head with the hilt of his sword. Tasinlo crumpled.

Tristan quickly and carefully put the three scroll cases into his travel-pack. But when he went to open the door, Jerold hissed. The sirnee sat, slowly switching his tail and sniffing the air. After a minute, he turned around and faced the door. Tristan opened it on an empty hallway. As Maria left, she heard a moan and turned back. Tasinlo was moving, trying to get up.

Tristan pulled her into the hallway and closed the door. He placed his palm over the wood, and when he moved away, wisps of smoke drifted up. He did the same with each door on their way to the stairs, and by the time they began climbing, two of the doors were in flames.

To the right of the staircase, hanging over the stone wall, was a large tapestry. Maria looked at it as she whispered.

"Yo-ray woeneeter sombear."

The cloth burst into flames. Tristan looked at Maria and opened his mouth.

"Fire!" yelled Maria. "Fire!"

Doors opened and people poured up the staircase. By

now, the entire tapestry was burning and the hallway was filling up with smoke. Bits of burning material dropped onto benches placed against the wall. Soon they would fuel the fire.

"Save the scrolls," yelled another voice.

Instead of leaving the building, Tristan ran after the apprentice calling to save the scrolls. He followed the man past the outside door and down another corridor. Maria ran close behind. The man entered a room and grabbed an armful of scrolls neatly stacked on wooden shelves. But when he turned to leave, he tripped over Jerold. The sirnee hissed and slashed out a front paw. The apprentice dropped the scrolls as he fell. Tristan helped him up and pushed him out the doorway in a single motion. Then he grabbed the stack of scrolls from the floor, closed his eyes, and tossed the scrolls back on the shelves. The room soon glowed red, and Tristan ran for the exit.

Maria stayed with him, and they joined the rest of the people streaming out the building. A bell began to ring. *There are no full magicians! No one will be able to use magic to put out the fire.* Maria looked at the people in the open space in front of the temple. Except for a few apprentices, most of them were nonmagicians. *They're dressed like us. No one will notice when we leave.* Tristan began shoving his way through the crowd and Maria held on to his shirt to keep them from being separated.

"Jerold. Where are you?" She heard him meow, but with all the people it was impossible to see him.

Down the road they went toward the gate. Maria saw armed guards taking up positions on both sides of the low wall surrounding the palace as people rushed out the door and ran toward the temple. In the middle of the crowd, three full magicians were pushing everyone aside. Tristan set a fast pace, but didn't run.

A second, different bell started ringing.

By the time the two of them got to the metal door securing that part of Casgarn, a small group of people were already there. The guard at the gate was arguing with a teenaged girl.

Jerold meowed loudly. Maria looked, but still couldn't see him. All she saw when she looked down were legs and feet.

"I told you, girl. I'm telling you all." The guard raised his voice. "You can't leave the palace compound. Don't you hear the alarm bell? You all know the rules. No one leaves until the all-clear trumpet sounds."

"But I have to go," said the girl. "I have orders from Lord Tajor. See, this is his mark!"

"I don't care whose orders you follow. I can't open the door until the trumpet sounds. Now get back to your room. All of you, get back to your rooms!"

Maria, who was standing a few feet behind the girl, grabbed Tristan's hand. All the people near the gate, except the two Kestrans — and the girl — turned back. As the pair watched, the girl moved behind the guard and hit him over the head with something she held in her hand. He fell; she rifled through his pocket. Within seconds, the girl had the key. But her hand trembled and the key wouldn't go into the gate lock. Tristan quickly stepped forward, touching the girl on the shoulder. Startled, she turned and raised her arm high. Tristan pointed to the lock; horns blared behind them; sounds of running feet pounding on stone filled the air.

Again, Tristan pointed to the lock. The girl slapped the key into his hand and Tristan quickly opened the door. The girl ran out first, but Maria turned her head when she had cleared the gate. "Jerold!" The sirnee raced into the grass. Tristan locked the door and threw the key away.

"Come on," said Maria, "We have to leave the city before they decide to raise the drawbridge. Jerold!"

"Aroo-eh." Maria saw him several feet ahead.

"Are you all right?"

"Rowl."

"Then let's go!"

The three ran. The sky behind them was lit with an orange haze as shouts of "The temple is burning! Fire! The temple!" rose in the air. When the trio reached the edge of the city, Maria stopped. The drawbridge was still down because a long line of packed wagons was slowly moving out of the city. But a company of soldiers was blocking the road, holding everyone else back.

"The city is safe!" said one of the men. "It's only the temple. The fire cannot spread. Go back to your homes."

Tristan pointed to the front of the line of soldiers. The girl who had hit the guard was there. Tristan pulled Maria forward.

Once again, the girl was arguing with a soldier. She held up the lord's silver mark and demanded to be allowed to leave the city. The soldier refused. The girl turned and looked into the city. Maria saw her face — it looked pale.

Tristan tapped Maria on the shoulder. He raised his

hand, holding his thumb and first finger together, making a circle.

"What's that?"

Tristan lifted an imaginary hood over his head and then pushed it off. He held out his hand, making the circle with his fingers again.

"Lord Jerbin's token."

Tristan nodded.

"You want me to show the soldier Jerbin's mark, too. Maybe he'll let the three of us out. She took out the token and ran to the girl. The soldier stopped talking and looked at Maria.

What am I going to say? How am I going to convince him to let us pass? Tasinlo said something — the king is leaving Casgarn. Maybe I can use that.

"Well, what do *you* want?"

Maria took a gamble. She looked at the girl and said, "Why are you still here? Your master sent you out an hour ago." Then Maria turned to the soldier, holding up her mark. "My master has also ordered the two of us to go. King Helborat will soon leave Casgarn and the messages we carry will ensure his safety. If you don't let us pass, you'll have to explain to our lords why you refused."

"If he keeps us here, he *must* support the prince," said the girl, after a short pause.

The word "prince," made the soldier snap to attention. "By order of Lord Tajor, these three will pass." When one of the other soldiers opened his mouth, the man repeated, "These three will pass!"

The soldiers parted — the girl ran, leaving Maria and Tristan to follow. She didn't stop at the end of the drawbridge, either. Maria saw her keep going toward the line of people making their way to the city.

"Meeeooww."

Maria looked; Jerold was several feet in front of them. "Let's go." They, too, walked rapidly down the road toward the refugees. An hour and a half later, when night had settled and the twin moons lit the sky, the three stopped and ate before falling asleep among the other travelers.

They rose early and, going against the flow of traffic, began their retreat. Tristan drew in the soil, telling Maria that he wanted to return to Felena. From there, they'd backtrack to the Thundrous Mountains.

Seven times in the following days, they changed direction and disappeared into the sea of people. Soldiers were everywhere, looking and searching for someone. Maria had no idea if the men were looking for her and Tristan, but somehow, she doubted it. "They can't know the scrolls were stolen because the temple burned. If Tasinlo escaped the fire, he won't say anything. If he did, the magicians will know he took the sacred scrolls and punish him. If he suspects us, which he probably does, he may think Lord Jerbin was behind the whole thing. In that case, he'll still keep quiet because he knows it would be his word against a full magician's."

Tristan nodded. Then he tapped the side of his head and touched Maria's in the same place.

"I never said I was stupid. I just said I wasn't a good magician.

Tristan looked into her eyes, shook his head, and again pretended to lower an imaginary hood over her head.

Jerold meowed, breaking them apart. When Maria looked up, she saw a magician–lord leading a large troop of men. They were headed toward the two, slowly riding through the crowd instead of alongside it. Tristan pushed Maria deeper into the line of refugees.

"Lord Tajor!" a soldier called out. "There's one."

The lord kicked his horse, forcing people to jump out of the way. "She's not the one," said a voice from inside the closed hood.

"Yes, Lord Tajor," snapped the soldier.

"Wait!" said the lord. "You, boy. Why are you here? Don't you know the king is raising another army to march into Kestra?"

"He is my brother, Master. He can't speak. That's why he is not in the army."

"He is not needed to speak, girl," snapped Tajor. "He is needed to fight."

"But, Master . . ."

"I have given an order, girl. If you are concerned about him, then join him. Our army is short of camp girls, too. There is much to be done that soldiers do not have time for. Look up, both of you!

"Tree-an dor no mus go jer rit."

Something slammed into Maria with the suddenness and force of a lightning bolt. Her body froze.

"You both will leave this line of useless people and walk north and east. In a few days, you will reach a river. Follow it northward until you come to the place where the new army trains. Present yourselves to the guard and inform

110

him that Lord Tajor has ordered you to serve your king." The magician–lord turned. "We must go! We're still no closer to finding the girl than before. We must find her, Captain. Since the scrolls were destroyed, she is now the key to our power."

"Yes, my Lord," snapped the captain. He waved his hands and the company moved out. One man dismounted and stood before Maria.

"You do understand me?"

Maria opened her mouth but it was hard for her to answer. *Yes,* she thought. *Say yes.* She concentrated on that simple task until her mouth moved and the sound "Yes," came out.

"Here," he said, holding a stack of journey cakes. "These will be enough until you both reach the river. Do you understand, girl?"

Again, Maria had to fight to say the simple answer.

"Good." The soldier put the food into her pack. He mounted, but before racing away to catch his captain called out. "You heard what the lord commanded. Go!"

Maria's left leg stepped forward; the right leg followed. People bumped her but her feet kept moving. She was out of line walking stiffly away from the road as a strange sort of silence invaded her mind. She could hear — the noisy refugees, her feet slapping on the hard earth. But the sounds were soft, muffled.

"Meow. Meow!"

But Maria couldn't see the sirnee. She saw nothing except what was eye-level in front of her.

Maria, stop yourself! What's wrong? What's happening? Why isn't my body listening? Why can't I control it? Wait

. . . control — that's it. Tajor put a spell on us! He's forcing us to obey him. Where's Tristan?

It took almost half a minute for Maria to turn her head far enough so she could see him. He was next to her with a blank stare on his face. She wanted to speak, but no matter what she did, she wasn't able to open her mouth. She tried to close her eyes but couldn't. *What's happening to me! Tristan, what should I do? I have to break the spell. But how?*

"Aroo-eh. Aroo-eh!"

She stared ahead: left foot, right foot, left foot. One step after another, each one taking her and Tristan farther away from Kestra and closer to the Yuniian army.

Chapter 11

Hours passed, and Maria couldn't think. Instead of trying to break the spell, she just listened to the rhythmic beat of her feet lifting up and down in a frightfully steady pattern. The two had just entered a wood; the leaves stopped the summer sun's burning rays.

Jerold cut in front, making her trip and fall. Once on the ground, she let out a deep breath. For the first time since Tajor enchanted her, she was able to close her eyes. She didn't hear Tristan's footsteps and assumed he had stopped.

"Meow."

Maria's eyes opened. *Jerold.*

The sirnee stared at Maria, his eyes wide open in the shadows. After a moment, Maria's arms stiffened; she tried to get up.

"Meow!" Maria stopped moving, her hands still clutching bits of dried leaves and dirt. Jerold lowered his head and rubbed it against Maria's hand. When she looked again, there was a smudge of dirt on his pink nose.

I have to break the spell. Jerold pushed his nose into her hand again. She squeezed her fist tighter and felt the earth grind in her palm. *I have to break free!* Slowly, Maria began to move her arms, trying to force them into the magician's cross.

"Burr. Burr." Jerold rubbed his cheek against her fist. Her arms stopped moving.

No! I have to do it my way. I have to make the magic fit me. But how?

Another thought drifted into her mind; one Maria didn't remember thinking. *Earrth . . . earrth.*

The elements of magic: earth — air, fire — water. They'll help me if I can make them listen. Earth is the most powerful. There's magic here if I can find it. Maria's head dropped an inch or so farther into the ground; her eyes closed. Tension in her arms and legs began to vanish. She felt her mind drifting . . . drifting down into the ground. *What did Lin say long ago? The difference between possible and impossible is the limit of your imagination.* It didn't matter to her that behind her closed eyes she actually felt as if she were under the ground. Now there were more impossibles. She saw tree roots growing up. She reached out and, not knowing if it were her real hand or one created in her imagination, touched the root. Her body tingled.

"Aroo-eh."

Break the spell, her mind whispered.

Her body shot up like a flying arrow. The spell was gone. The compulsion to blindly obey had vanished. She looked and saw Tristan, standing perfectly still, staring straight ahead, waiting for her. "Tristan," she shouted, getting up. "Tristan!" She shook his shoulders and yelled in his ear. "Break the spell, Tristan. Concentrate. Please!"

But nothing happened. He continued to stare straight

ahead and Maria forced him to sit. "Tristan, think of the magic. You do it better than I do, you know that. Listen, try to break the spell!" Slowly, his shoulders relaxed and his eyes closed. Maria watched him take several deep breaths. When his eyes finally opened, the glazed look was gone from them.

"Are you all right?"

He slowly nodded.

"I did it, Tristan. Don't ask me how because I don't know. I listened to Lin. I let my imagination carry me. It was almost as if . . . as if my mind floated away from my body. I know that's impossible, but that's what it felt like. I thought *to* the magic. Do you hear? I thought directly to the magic and asked it to release me from the spell. And it did!"

The first thing they did was eat everything the soldier had given them. As they finished, Maria heard a muffled meow and saw Jerold coming with a young rabbit. While Tristan prepared it, she sat near the fire she started, feeling its warmth, and petting Jerold, who lay sleepily purring in her lap.

After they ate, they decided to stay in that patch of woods for the rest of the day. "Do you remember the ground we walked over after the magician put that spell on us?"

Tristan shook his head.

"I think we crossed several farm fields before entering these woods. But I'm not sure. I'm not even sure which way Felena is anymore. Do you still want to go back that way?" Tristan shrugged his shoulders before he lay down near the fire and slept.

In the morning when Maria woke up, she saw that Jerold must have hunted for them again because breakfast, a midsized chicken, was already cooking. "It means there are farms near here," she said, sitting up and combing her hair with her fingers. "Have you decided how to get back to Kestra?" He shook his head.

After breakfast, Maria looked at Jerold. "Do you remember where we entered these woods?"

"Rowl." Jerold just sat, licking his paw and wiping his face.

"Well, show us." The sirnee walked away, backtracking until they stood at the edge of the trees. There were farm fields, and even though it was early, people were working in them. Tristan shook his head, looked at Maria, and headed into the trees again.

"I guess we're not going back to Felena." In two hours, they left the woods, walking east. When Maria asked where he was going, he made a snakelike motion, then rubbed his palms over his face as if he were washing it.

"You're going to find the river that the magician–lord told us about." Tristan nodded and then pointed south. "Do you think that's the best way?"

Tristan faced in the direction they came from. He pretended to slip a hood off his head, then moved his legs up and down as if he were on a horse.

"Maybe you're right. The magicians were looking for someone and there were a lot of soldiers on the road leading to Casgarn. We can't be worse off heading this way."

The path they were following soon disappeared as the ground rose and fell in gentle rolling hills. Farmers worked patches of ground here and there, and the two steered clear when they saw anyone. They passed no woods, and both lunch and supper were whatever they stole from untended fields. For several days they traveled this way, taking unripened food they needed and staying away from people. Jerold hunted, but all he had been able to find since they had left the woods was one chicken and a small rabbit. Early on the third day, the land flattened, becoming rocky and unused. Jerold meowed and raced ahead when he saw the leading edge of a forest. Shortly after entering it they came to the river.

Everyone took a long drink, then turned south. The river was wide and slow, winding its way through the trees. After an hour, Maria rounded a curve and saw three buildings, a large dock that held five empty barges, and several potas, small canoes made out of hollow logs.

"Rowl."

Tristan pulled her behind the trees. He stared at the buildings, looking for signs of life, but didn't see any. Motioning Maria to stay where she was, both Tristan and Jerold disappeared into the trees. Maria lost sight of them. Soon she saw Tristan peering into one of the windows. He moved from window to window, carefully looking into each. When he was satisfied that the lodge was really deserted, he stood in the open and waved for her.

Together, they walked into the largest of the three buildings. "Wow!" said Maria. The inside of the building was a mess. Furniture was turned over everywhere, and the material covering the wooden couch and chairs was torn open. Broken plates and spoiled food covered the floor.

"Whoever left here, left in one big hurry." They walked through the rest of the house; all the rooms were in the same state of disarray. Nothing they saw was whole; everything was in at least two pieces.

They explored the other two houses; everything in them was destroyed too. "Someone was looking for something. I wonder what?" Tristan shook his head.

As they left the last house, they saw Jerold sitting in the clearing. A fat duck was lying at his feet. "I wouldn't mind having a good meal for a change. We could probably salvage enough from the torn mattresses to make up sleeping mats, too. What do you think? Can we camp here?"

Tristan nodded as he headed for the dead bird.

For the rest of the day, they did nothing except take a long bath in the river, eat several times — since hunting was good — and sit by the water. Once, Tristan took out one of the scrolls. They both looked at it, but neither could read the strange language or recognize any words. Tristan shook his head as he carefully rolled the scroll up and replaced it in its case.

When the sun began to set, they decided to go to sleep. Tristan carried loose straw from several torn mattresses into the large house and onto the kitchen floor. The small houses had only one door; the large one two, the second leading out of the kitchen. As it turned out, his caution paid off.

Maria woke when she felt something on her chest. "Mrrr. Mrrr." She stretched. "Aroo-eh!"

"All right. I'm awake." She rose and looked out the window. It was late. A tree growing outside had kept the room dark but the sun was well up. As she stood by the window, she heard the sounds of horses.

"Tristan! Someone's coming!"

Tristan was instantly alert; in seconds his pack was on his back. He pulled Maria toward the main room, and they looked cautiously out of the window.

Into the clearing rode a company of eight soldiers. Leading them was a man wearing a dirty robe that had once been pink. Though a bandage was wrapped around his forehead, Maria recognized him immediately. *Tasinlo!* "How did he find us? He couldn't have followed our tracks."

Tristan looked at her sharply, putting a finger to his lips.

The men stopped in the clearing. "What is this place?" they heard Tasinlo ask.

"It was an overnight stop for trade barges, Apprentice. The owners sided with the prince and the place is deserted now," came the answer.

"Search it, Sergeant!"

"What makes you think the two who started the fire are here? If they were, they must have heard our horses and would have run into the forest. Shouldn't we look for tracks leading away?"

"In no lu-ter ah see!"

shouted Tasinlo.

The freezing spell! thought Maria as she turned to look at Tristan. But he just smiled back at her. "His magic didn't work."

"Now, if they are here, they are frozen," said Tasinlo.

"But Apprentice, even I know that the spell works only as long as it is heard. If they are hiding near here and were frozen, they are no longer because you have stopped chanting."

"Do you presume to teach me my craft! Though I wear the pink now, within the year I shall be a full magician, two years before my apprenticeship should end. I have changed the spell and added words I believe will freeze the two I search for until *I* release them."

"You believe?"

"Your belief is not required, Sergeant. All I require is that you follow my orders."

"But Apprentice, the king's new army marches south. We are needed there."

"I have told you before. I am Tasinlo, apprentice to Lord Re-in, and in his absence, I speak for him. Do you dare disobey me?"

The sergeant took a deep breath and shook his head. "No, Apprentice," he said as he exhaled. "But I am reminding you that you have ordered us away from our duties. Be warned that when we return I will report to the camp commander. If there are penalties to suffer, it will be you, and the lord you speak for, who bears them. Are you sure they were here?"

"No-trun-depor entay,"
said Tasinlo.

"No-trun-depor entay."

Then he leaned forward and searched the outside of the houses with a slow, steadily moving head.

"Well, *Apprentice*. Were they here?"

"I don't know!" One of the soldiers snickered — Tasinlo turned furiously. "Who did that! Who laughs at the king's magic?" No one answered.

"They don't laugh at the magic, Apprentice. They laugh at . . ."

"Do you see the Uter River?" shouted Tasinlo. "Magic is difficult. If it weren't, every peasant from here to Ekloy would be doing it. It's even more difficult near running water. But it was my seeking spell that led us here, remember that. Now Sergeant, I have ordered you to search these buildings!"

"Meow. Meow!" The sirnee was standing on the beginnings of a forest path. As soon as Tasinlo saw him, Jerold ran into the trees.

"I told you they were near. That's their cat. Follow me!" He kicked his horse and the men vanished between the trees.

Tristan waited until the last echoes of the horses disappeared before leading Maria out the back door. When he started into the woods, Maria called him back.

"Tristan, did you ever hear of magic being affected by water? Tasinlo said that running water made casting magic harder."

Tristan looked at the river as he shook his head.

"Neither have I. And I never heard of a seeking spell other than the one I used to find you the first time. But that only works when a person is close and we saw no bubble of light. It can't be the same spell. Even the words are different."

Tristan shrugged his shoulders and turned back toward the forest.

"Wait. Don't you understand what a seeking spell like that means? Tasinlo followed us. If we go into the woods, he'll eventually catch us. Even if he's not a very good magician, we can't fight the soldiers. Maybe we should . . ."

Tristan looked at her.

"Maybe we should split up? You head south toward Kestra. I'll go north. That will confuse Tasinlo. You'll have a better chance if you're alone."

Tristan stepped closer to her and slowly shook his head. A second later, he smiled. Taking her hand, he ran to the water.

"I don't understand," said Maria. But when he untied one of the potas, she did. "We'll take a pota. If Tasinlo's magic has trouble working near running water, he might not find us. We have to ask Befany when we get back about that. I don't understand why their magic is affected by water; Eonoway's never was."

Again, Tristan shrugged his shoulders, then helped Maria into the pota. Just as he pushed off, they heard a meow. Running toward them was Jerold. He reached the edge of the dock and jumped, landing gracefully. He looked first at Maria, then at Tristan. "Rowl." The sirnee settled himself on Maria's travel-pack.

"Jerold, nothing about you is normal. Sirnees may look and sound like cats, but they aren't cats. Eonoway said sirnees were a special breed. I think you're a different animal altogether. What do you have to say about that?"

"Aroo-eh." Jerold curled up into a ball.

"Well, cats don't act as decoys and lead people away," she said to Tristan as he shook his head.

Three hours later they were still paddling. Several times they stopped and listened for sounds of horses, but they never heard anything. When it was time to rest, Maria told Tristan to head for the eastern shore. Tasinlo was on the western side, and his seeking spell would have to cross water to find them.

As they ate, Maria thought about everything Eonoway had ever told her. *Why do the Yuniian magicians have trouble casting magic across water? Kestra's magicians don't because I've seen Eonoway perform her spells over water. What's the difference between the magic of Yunii and Kestra? What am I missing?* Maria couldn't answer her own questions, so she finished her lunch in silence.

Much later, when they were both exhausted and the sun was at the edge of the sky, Maria heard faint sounds coming from downriver. Trumpets. Yuniian army trumpets. Yuniian army trumpets getting louder each time they sounded.

Chapter 12

Tristan hit the side of the pota to get Maria's attention, then pointed toward the eastern shore. On reaching land, they carried the pota away from the exposed shoreline into the trees thirty or forty feet away. Maria abruptly sat down, breathing heavily.

The trumpets sounded again. They were even closer than before.

"They're on our side of the river. We have to put the pota back. We have to get to the other shore!" But when she stood, the trumpets they had just heard were answered by another blast. The second blare was farther away, but close enough for Maria to tell it came from the other side of the river.

Tristan held up two fingers.

"I know. Soldiers are on both sides. What do we do?"

Tristan pointed from the pota to the river.

"We can't get back in now. They'll see us."

"Meow." Jerold called from the trees.

But Tristan didn't listen to the sirnee or Maria. Two sets of trumpets blew in the near distance while he lifted his end of the pota. Maria wearily lifted hers, and together, they hauled it back to the water. But when Maria tried to get in, he wouldn't let her, wading instead several feet out and pushing the empty pota into the current. Then he and Maria ran for the trees.

"Meow!"

Tristan touched Maria and pointed. They started running after Jerold. After only a few minutes, Maria stopped. Breathing quickly, she punched out the next words, "I have to rest." But there was no time.

"Aroo-eh!"

The trumpets sounded again. The soldiers were closer. Tristan and Maria headed deeper into the forest. Jerold stayed in front, meowing whenever he changed directions. The trumpets on the far side of the river became softer. The nearer ones didn't.

"Listen!" They stopped. Above the sound of their labored breathing, Maria heard them — "Horses!"

"Meow!"

Maria looked around but Jerold was gone.

"Me-ow!" Jerold cried again.

"Where are you?" said Maria, eyes frantically searching.

The third time he called, Maria looked up and saw the sirnee in a tree.

Tristan smiled. He ran to Maria, lifting her so she could reach the lowest branch. Then he pushed her feet up. Once Maria started climbing, Tristan took a running jump and reached the branch Maria had just left. He was a good climber and was soon on the branch next to her — then above her.

Maria looked down. In the hazy dusk, she could still see the forest floor. Tristan's feet disappeared into the leaves, but reaching for the next branch to follow, she lost her balance. Her arms flayed against the air and she tumbled backward. Maria tried not to scream but when her head slammed into a branch, she let out a cry. Her body hit the ground with a thud.

I have to . . . get up. I have to . . . get away! She rose and took a step. *My head! I can't . . . stay here.* She stumbled a few feet forward and fell down unconscious.

Maria became aware of her pounding head. She remained still, eyes closed, listening to the burning wood. Muffled sounds of men eating and talking drifted toward her. Footsteps came near; rough hands snapped her head from side to side. She wanted to cry out but didn't.

"She's still out," said a voice above her.

"She will wake soon enough," answered another. "Then she'll tell me what I want to know."

"Is she that important, Lord Weedna?"

"She may be, Captain," answered the lord. There was a long pause and then the voice continued. "Some time ago one of my apprentices came to me with grave news. The temple at Casgarn was burned and our scrolls were destroyed."

"Even the sacred ones, my Lord?"

"Yes, Captain, even the sacred ones."

"But that means . . ."

"Yes, Captain. With the scrolls gone, apprentices can never be fully trained until we rewrite the spells we know. Also, magician–lords cannot further their knowledge or look up spells they have forgotten. This is a disaster, one we may never recover from. Now, more than ever, we must find the key and restore the ancient magic, magic without spells."

Magic without spells? How is that . . .

"But what does this girl have to do with the fire or the search?"

"When I met Tasinlo on the other side of the Uter River, he told me about a girl and her silent brother. They said they were on an errand for Lord Jerbin, and after seeing Jerbin's token, Tasinlo let them into the temple. Shortly after that, the fire started. Tasinlo believes they were the ones who started it. Since the king will not call off his attack on Prince Chan, it is up to Lord Olsten and me to find the two Tasinlo chases. He said they were in this area."

"We didn't find a boy, my Lord."

"The blood was still dripping from the girl when you found her so her accident was recent. If the boy is hiding near us, we'll find him in the morning."

Maria's mouth opened and before she could stop herself, she coughed. Hands gripped her shoulders and pulled. Everything swam in rapid circles as she leaned heavily against the man behind her. But he firmly pushed her forward. Maria stumbled toward the fire, staying erect until she was almost there. Then she slipped to her knees; her hands dropped to the ground.

Lord Weedna spoke. "Look at me, girl!"

Maria opened her eyes but kept her head level so all she could see was a man's feet and the bottom half of a red robe.

"I said, look at me!"

Maria raised her head until she looked into the eyes of Lord Weedna. His hood was off, but with only the firelight dancing across his face, it was impossible to tell what he looked like. The tone in his voice, however, was the same as Lord Jerbin's.

"What is your name?"

"Maria."

"You will address me as befits my station, girl."

Maria tried to think, but the throbbing pain beat against her forehead. She didn't answer and lowered her head. The pain eased a little.

Lord Weedna stepped closer to Maria. "Captain," he said. Maria was hauled to her feet again. "You will answer and tell me everything I wish to know! Where are you going?

"Eewow gerinta sinkrata discot."

The truth . . . Maria could not finish her thought. The pain beating on the inside of her head was joined with another sensation. Her muscles tensed. *I have to talk to this man . . . I have to tell him what he wants to know.* Maria tried to look at him but he kept moving around. She swallowed. Just as she opened her mouth, she heard a faint sound from the forest behind her.

"Meow."

"I . . . am . . . Ma . . . ri . . . a . . . I . . . am . . . go . . . ing . . ."

The pain returned and Maria almost fell. The hands holding her up squeezed into her shoulders but she hardly felt them.

"Speak, girl. I command it!"

A thought drifted into her head. *Earrth . . . airr . . . fiirre . . . waater. Seeek the fourr. Seeek the maagic.*

Maria's legs gave way; she fell. Lord Weedna said something because no one pulled her up. She sat, head down, hands on the ground. The urge to speak was gone, and she took long, deep breaths.

"Here's some water," said a voice. One of her hands was lifted; she felt a cup placed in it. She drank. The water tasted cool and fresh. Her mind cleared. She kept her eyes closed, gripping the ground with her other hand.

Think of the four, she thought. Her mind wandered. Without her realizing, it left her body as peacefully as smoke leaving a fire. Her mind felt the cool breeze against her cheek. It felt the water of the gently flowing river. It felt the hard ground and the warmth of the hot coals under the flames. She drank the rest of the water and was only partly aware when someone took away the cup. "Four . . . four," she whispered to herself. Her body tingled.

"Aroo."

"Now, girl," said Lord Weedna, "Talk. Who are you? Where are you going?

"Eewow gerinta sinkrata discot."

The truth spell made her head snap up, forcing her to look at Lord Weedna. Her mouth opened — her mind returned to her body. "I . . . am . . . Ma . . ." *Fight it! Fight his magic!* Pain beat inside her head. "Ri . . . a . . . I . . . am . . ."

Seek the fourr again. Bee one wiith them.

Her mind reached and melded with the elements. The tingles returned.

"Aroo-eh."

Her urge to speak was gone. The part of Maria's mind that wasn't fighting the pain knew she could say whatever she wanted. But she couldn't let Lord Weedna know. She started speaking again. "I . . . am . . . go . . . ing . . . to . . . Kes . . . tra."

"Kestra!" said Lord Weedna. "Why?"

"I . . . was . . . told . . . to . . . go . . . to . . . the . . . li . . . brar . . . y . . . and . . . then . . . stay . . . in . . . Kes . . . tra . . . un . . . til . . . the . . . war . . . is . . . o . . . ver."

"Who was the boy with you? Where is he now?"

Maria took a breath. She was becoming tired. "He . . . is . . . my . . . friend . . . I . . . do . . . not . . . know . . . where . . . he . . . is . . . we . . . sep . . . a . . . rat . . . ed."

"Who told you to burn the temple!"

Maria's head drooped. Both hands dug into the ground.

"Blast this water!" shouted Lord Weedna.

"Eewow gerinta sinkrata discot!"

"Who told you to burn the temple?"

Maria's mind raced. She tried to think. Suddenly, some-one pulled her hair, forcing her head up. "Lord . . . Jer . . . bin."

"Jerbin!"

When the hand released her, Maria fell all the way to the ground. She heard Lord Weedna shouting orders.

"Captain, dispatch a runner immediately to King Helborat. Inform him that there may be a conspiracy among his full magicians. They may be seeking to solve the riddle for themselves! With the scrolls destroyed, the ancient magic will be the key to our future power. Tell him if the power is not shared, there will be a new king in Casgarn. Helborat must return to the capital."

"Yes, Lord Weedna."

"Send another runner to Lord Olsten. Tell him what you heard. Have him join me with all his men as soon as possible. We must find and confront Jerbin together."

"Yes, my Lord."

The last thing Maria heard before she fainted was running feet and the neighing of horses.

Maria became semiconscious when she was picked up and thrown in the back of a wagon. Her head screamed, though very little came out of her mouth. The camp was broken; everyone rode. It was not an easy trip for Maria. Each time the wagon rolled over a rock or branch, she bounced. It was impossible to rest. The pain never went away; it only varied from a great deal to a little bit. In the early morning, she felt the ground move. It took her a moment to realize that she was on a barge crossing the river. She closed her eyes and finally fell into a deep sleep as the flat boat gently rocked her.

When she woke, she was lying on the ground in front of the large building she and Tristan had been hiding in when they saw Tasinlo. *Tristan!* She sat up. The building swam around her ... she closed her eyes and swayed until the pain went away. This time she opened her eyes slowly, and the building didn't move. Everything was the same as when they had left. *Where's Tristan?* She saw a bucket of water near her and moved to it. That's when she noticed her ankle was securely tied to a tree, but there was enough room for her to reach the water. As she drank, she thought and tried to remember what had happened the night before. *I lied to Lord Weedna when he put a truth spell on me. I remember talking ... and the pain stopped me. I remember his yelling at the water and saying the spell again. How could I have fought the spell? Wait ... I know. The pain ... the weak spell because of the water. That's what helped me. It wasn't anything I did. How could I have fought the magic of a full magician?*

The water helped ease the pain, and the bread one of the soldiers brought her a few minutes later helped even more. After she ate, she slept. No one bothered her the rest of the day as she slept and woke, slept and woke. Soldiers raced in and out of the camp, and when another red-robed lord appeared, Lord Weedna greeted him, then the two disappeared into the main house. When Maria finally woke up, feeling that her head was part of her body again, it was night. The twin moons were overhead, Pern, as always, circling his big brother. The wind was blowing; clouds were rapidly filling the dark sky.

Maria stretched and drank from the bucket someone had refilled. Next to it, on a flat stone, were bread and two wide strips of meat. She ate and drank. As she did, she looked carefully at the knot tied around her foot. It was bound too tightly to loosen. She crawled back to the tree and sat, leaning up against it. *Don't come for me, Tristan.*

Get the scrolls back to Befany. Maybe they will help her free Lin; maybe they will help Andraya defeat the Yuniian armies.

Tristan didn't answer. But a soft mew from the darkness behind her did.

Chapter 13

As the first drops of rain starting falling, Maria felt a light touch behind her. Jerold was rubbing his cheek against her side. Then he walked on her lap and began kneading his paws, in-out, in-out, pushing into her legs. All the while Maria petted him and listened to the soothing sound of his purrs. When he stopped, she picked him up and kissed him. *You came after me. Oh Jerold, you came for me!* He remained in her arms for a brief minute while she hugged him, but then began to squiggle. Maria put him down and scratched the side of his head. Jerold stood but remained balanced in her lap. His head lowered and turned, pressing against Maria's fingers. When his hind legs pushed up and Maria moved, he toppled over on his side.

Maria picked him up and hugged him again. "I love you, Jerold."

"Mrrr. Mrrr." The sirnee wiggled out of her arms, walked to Maria's foot and began chewing on the knot. She watched him silently cutting away the knot one strand at a time as the light drizzle became heavier. When Jerold finished, Maria was free.

She remained still, looking out over Lord Weedna's

camp. Fires hissed and burned low; men with blankets draped over them walked back and forth. Despite the rain, the soldiers continued to pace, guarding the sleeping camp.

Jerold sat watching. His ears moved — first their tips pointed toward Maria; next to the side; last to the back. He was listening. He stood and shook, throwing off drops of water. The rain was heavy now, and both he and Maria were soaked. The sirnee walked away, disappearing into the wet woods.

One of the guards passed Maria but made no move toward her. Though he carried a sputtering torch, there was not enough light to see that the rope was only draped over her foot. She waited until the soldier vanished into the night before slipping away.

Maria had been at the northern end of the camp and Jerold, who had waited for her, led her farther north. After a few minutes, the sirnee stopped. He meowed once, and Maria turned when she heard a noise over the rain. "Tristan!"

He immediately lifted his hand and placed one finger across her lips. Then he silently hugged her. When they broke apart, Tristan began walking back toward the camp. The forest was almost black — a heavy layer of clouds hid all light from the twin moons, and the growing wind whipped the leaves back and forth.

When they reached the edge of the camp, Tristan kneeled down and began crawling on the soggy grass that grew between the edge of the forest and river bank. He was heading for the dock and motioned Maria to follow. As soon as she cleared the treeline, the wind tried to push her back into the trees. Maria dropped lower, putting her chest into the quickly growing puddles. Jerold, standing in paw-deep water, meowed; Maria kept going.

Lightning flashed, and for an instant the sky was day bright. Maria quickly pulled the sirnee closer to her and both remained motionless. When the darkness returned, they continued crawling. At the land's edge, the river was lashing the shore. Tristan had pulled one of the potas close enough for Maria to step into. Jerold jumped first, and as soon as Maria was in, Tristan pushed off, taking his place in the back of the pota.

In the open water, the wind spun them around like a child's top. Tristan tried desperately to straighten the pota, but couldn't. He banged on the side and pointed to the paddle. As Maria reached, another bolt of lightning fell. In the sudden light, the pota, black against the foaming white water, was clearly visible. When the night returned, a trumpet sounded.

By now they were past the camp, almost in the center of the raging river. Maria rowed until her arms were exhausted; her head ached and the pain of the night before returned. But she didn't give up. "One, two — one, two," she said to herself as she stroked again and again, helping to keep the bow of the pota pointed straight ahead. The pota raced onward; time passed. All at once the sound of the roaring wind was overtaken by another sound. Maria heard a rumbling noise in the distance. She looked behind, pointing to the shore. Rowing together, they tried to turn the pota. Maria's arms moved, but there was no force in them.

The pota began spinning again and even Tristan had no strength left to steer. He put his paddle down and let the river carry the pota where it wanted. He pulled Maria into the center.

"Meow! Meow!"

The pota began spinning faster and faster. The low rumbling became louder. Waves reached up and water poured in. Tristan wrapped his arms around Maria and they huddled down together. Jerold pushed his way between the two.

Lightning lit the sky — thunder crashed over them. Immediately afterward, the pota slammed into something. Maria heard wood splitting as water flooded over her. She screamed as the river pulled her into itself. Her arms beat against the water as she tried to keep her head up.

Again lightning showed her the landscape rushing past. The river had narrowed, and torrents of water swirled and bubbled as they were forced between cliffs that had appeared on both banks. "Tristaaan!" Maria went over a small waterfall, dropping four or five feet. Her chest slammed into the riverbed, forcing the air out of her lungs. The river pulled her forward; her head reached the surface.

The wind blew, the rain continued, and lightning crisscrossed the sky. But the river slowed. Thunder echoed through the trees that reappeared along its sides as Maria's strength gave out. Water forced itself down her throat and she coughed. Her arms moved weakly, just barely keeping her head above water. *He shouldn't have come back for me* she thought as the water pulled her under. *He would have been safe . . .*

She struggled for air.

Seeek the maagic.

Her mind drifted. It touched the water, the wet ground,

the whistling wind. Her arms moved and lifted her head above the water. She gasped as air filled her lungs.

"Murrp!"

She was filled with a strange energy. Tingles came — she swam toward the eastern shore. Something scraped her knees, and when she put her feet down, they touched bottom. The water pushed her sideways and she fell, but when she put her hands out to break her fall, they too, hit bottom. She half walked, half crawled out of the river. Maria was exhausted and wanted nothing more than to collapse. But she didn't. She continued until she reached the shelter of the first few trees before falling.

Singing birds woke her. She moved her arms and legs, stretched, and felt her still soaking dress clinging to her. Maria sat up. Her head hurt, but the pain was dull compared to the pounding of last night. She looked around, and through the trees, saw the sun drying out the land and the river once again a gentle highway.

Tristan! She stood, and the sudden movement made her head swirl. She held a tree for support. "Tristan! Tristaaan!" Nothing but the fluttering of startled birds answered. Nothing but bird sounds and a soft mew at her feet.

"Jerold! You didn't drown! Oh Jerold!" Maria bent down and picked up the sirnee, burying her face in his damp fur. "Tristan," she whispered. "Did he make it? How are we going to find him?"

Maagic.

Maria dropped Jerold as if his fur had become sharp quills. The sirnee landed on his feet and looked up.

138

"Who said that?" She turned around but couldn't see anyone. "Who's there?" she called.

Thiink.

"Who said that!" Her body shook and it wasn't from the damp dress. Someone was there, close enough to whisper, but invisible to her eyes. "Where are you?" she shouted, and this time, she waited for the echo of her voice to disappear before looking deeper between the trees. She saw nothing. Slowly, she slipped down. "There's no one here, Jerold."

Thiink of the maagic.

Maria pressed her hands against her ears. "This can't be happening!" she said to the sirnee who came and sat in her lap. "I hear him . . . I hear a voice. But no one's there. It can't be real. How can I hear someone who's not here? It's impossible!"

Wiith maagic, nothiing is imposssible.

"Stop it! What's happening to me? Who are you? How are you doing this?" But there was only silence.

Maria stood, catching Jerold off guard and forcing him to twist in the air so he could land on his feet. She ran deeper into the woods, stopping and looking behind trees, between trees, beyond trees. But each time, the only thing she saw was more trees. "Am I going crazy?" she said to Jerold. But the sirnee just looked at her.

Maria stopped, thought the words of her calming spell, and relaxed. Then it hit her. She hadn't recited the spell; she had thought it. And it had worked. *I thought the spell and it worked! That means Eonoway WAS wrong! It is possible to think to the magic.*

"But I knew that," she said to herself. "Tristan does real magic without speaking." She remembered when . . . what was his name . . . Jeffrey, the boy with the shape-changing girl, told her Tristan had healed her arm. She remembered Tristan drawing the box with the hole in it and her deciding that Lin was right. Her feet were not the same size as Eonoway's. *I have to find my own way of doing magic, but I haven't tried very hard to do that yet.* "I have power, Jerold. Eonoway told me that. And I've used it! I just never thought about it before." She sat, leaning against the tree.

Now her mind raced. She thought about the spell Lord Tajor had placed on her when he forced her walk to the army. She had broken it. *But how? What did I say to Tristan? It was . . . as if my mind left my body. Yes! My mind did leave. It felt the roots of the nearby trees . . . and I tingled with . . . power. I connected with the earth, the first element. I thought to the magic, told it to break the spell, and it did.*

She remembered Lord Weedna. *The same thing happened! My mind floated, felt the ground, the wind, the fire, and water. It touched all of them! But how did I get the magic to listen to me without saying any spells? What did Lord Weedna say? Ancient magic that works without reciting spells. Can it really work? Did I find a new way of . . .*

Beeleeve. Beeleeve!

Maria twisted around — again no one was there. But she didn't have time to be frightened. She knew that something important was happening, more important than figuring out who was playing tricks with her. "Believe," she whispered. "What did Eonoway say to me? To be a true magician I have to believe in myself."

140

Maria thought her calming spell again. She placed her hands on the ground; her fists tightened. Jerold meowed but she ignored the sirnee. "I have to do it. I have to feel the magic." She concentrated on the ground — forced her mind to see it behind her eyes. It happened — dark, rich, forest soil surrounded her. She breathed deeply and smelled the air. The breeze was gentle as it brushed lightly against her cheeks. She heard the water and forced her mind toward it. Chills sped along her arms, across her chest, and around her neck. Her body shuddered.

"Rowl."

Tristan, where are you?

Suddenly, an image appeared in her mind. Tristan lying face up, eyes closed, chest moving in a slow, steady rhythm.

"Aroo-eh!" Jerold sprang away and ran along the river bank, heading farther south.

Maria followed. "Wait for me!" But Jerold kept running. Soon her legs tired and a pain began to grow in her chest, but Maria ignored it and continued chasing after her sirnee. Ten minutes later, Maria saw him. "Tristan! Tristan!"

Tristan looked up at the first sound. He pushed himself up as Maria ran into him with her arms open. She crushed him in an embrace but hardly felt his arms returning it. She broke away and looked at him.

He half smiled as he held her hand a moment. Then he let go.

"What's the matter, Tristan? You're alive. I'm alive. It's a miracle, but we both survived."

Tristan lowered his head and pointed to his travel-pack.

The back of it had opened and most of the contents were gone. The ancient scrolls had been eaten by the river.

"It's all right," she said, pulling him back to the nearest tree and sitting. "We don't need the scrolls to free Lin."

Tristan looked at her and tilted his head.

"I've found something. I've found a way to make the magic listen to me. Together with Befany, we can free Lin ourselves. I can talk to the magic. Do you hear me, Tristan. I can talk to the magic!"

But when Tristan looked at her, she couldn't tell him what she had discovered. They both heard horses pounding along the riverbank.

Chapter 14

Tristan turned toward the forest and began trotting.

"I can't run. I still hurt from following Jerold."

He slowed. Soon the river was lost behind rows of trees, and when they heard the horses coming, they dropped down. Soldiers were racing along the shoreline.

"If they're looking for the pota," said Maria as they got up, "they may have a long ride ahead of them."

Tristan just stared at her. The spark in his eyes was gone. For the first time since they met, his black eyes held no mystery. They were just eyes. *He's given up.*

He began walking without waiting for her.

"Aroo-eh. Aroo-eh."

Maria wrapped her hands around the closest tree and concentrated. *Make him stop,* she thought to the magic. But Tristan kept going. Then he turned back, saw her, and waved for her to follow. *I have to do it!* Maria closed her eyes, felt the bark against her cheek, and willed her mind into the wood — it entered the tree and descended into the earth.

"Aroo-eh."

It touched the magic.

Tristan, stop. Don't give up. We'll free Lin.

Wha . . . wha . . .

Maria's eyes opened. She heard . . . Tristan stood a dozen feet away, staring.

"Did you . . . did you hear me?"

Tristan slowly nodded.

Tristan! I spoke to the magic but you heard me. We . . .

How . . . how? thought Tristan.

Maria ran to him. "And I heard you! We spoke to each other! Do you realize what we've done. We mind-spoke! Lin *was* right. You remember the block of wood he had? I just figured out how to speak to the magic. I know how to get my words through the hole. I did it before but I never knew I had. Now I know and I'll show you and Befany. We don't need the scrolls to free Lin. We can do it ourselves." *I promise, the three of us will free Lin.*

Tristan just stared at her. *Can . . . you . . . hear . . . me?*

"Yes."

Tristan didn't move. His arms froze in the air as his hands reached for her cheeks. His legs shook. His eyes reddened. *You . . . can . . . hear . . . me.*

Maria nodded. Tristan's eyes sparkled. But the king's soldiers would not let them have their minute of discovery alone. They had returned, calling to each other, spreading out and looking for tracks.

Tristan took her hand and walked. The shouting grew. The walk became a trot. Someone yelled. The trot became a jog. Horses entered the forest. The jog became a run.

I can't run! thought Maria when the pain in her chest re-

144

turned. But Tristan never turned or looked at her. *Can't you hear me?* Tristan didn't answer as he held her hand tighter and sped up. "Stop!" she called, dropping to her knees.

Tristan wildly looked around. When he saw a large pine tree, he pushed her toward it. The bottom branch was low and wide and welcomed them as if it knew they needed a place to hide. Tristan reached the trunk and pointed up. Jerold went first; they followed.

Maria clamped her lips together when the old pine's needles stuck her. She inched herself upward, ignoring the tiny pinpicks and sticky sap that clung to her hands, arms, and legs. When they were high above the ground, and completely hidden, they stopped. The shouting men came closer. Tristan pushed Maria, forcing her to inch closer to the trunk. He was making sure she didn't fall.

"Do you see them?" a voice shouted.

"Their tracks led this way," said another.

"There's nothing here," shouted a third voice from the distance. "Either we lost them or they're in one of these blasted trees."

"If they are," answered the first voice, "we'll never see them. Too many leaves."

"Lord Weedna will find them," said the third voice. "We know they were here; their tracks led away from the water. The lord's magic will find them. Josta, Penstil, Thomas, Rehay. Spread out and search the area. I'll ride back to lead the lord here. If you find their tracks, two of you follow and two wait. I'll be back in a few hours."

"Yes, Sergeant," answered a new voice.

Maria heard one horse run off, and when the sound of its hooves disappeared, she heard the other four horses as they started making slow wide circles.

Do you think it's safe to try to sneak away? she thought. But as before, Tristan didn't answer. *Why don't you answer me!* her mind shouted. But Tristan didn't hear. Instead, he crept along the branch and looked down. *It worked last time. Why can't he hear me? Why won't the magic listen to me now?*

Jerold nudged his head into her. Then he stretched, exposing his sharp, curved claws. Before retracting them, he scratched the outside layer of the bark covering the branch. When Maria didn't pay any attention to him, he nudged her again. "Brrr. Brrr."

What's the matter with you? She petted him with one hand but held tightly to the tree trunk with the other.

Jerold just meowed and tried to sit in her lap.

The tree . . . when I mind-spoke to Tristan, I was holding onto that small tree. Why is that important? What does Jerold want to tell me? Wait! I used the tree to help my mind reach the earth — to reach the magic.

Maria closed her eyes and forced her mind outward. It was a little easier this time; she didn't have to push so hard. Her mind shifted — it felt the huge tree, entered it, and went down. She gripped the branch tighter, moving as close to the trunk as possible to keep from falling. But she kept concentrating, kept her mind traveling toward the first element. She reached it; magic flowed into her.

"Brrr."

Tristan, can you hear me?

146

Yes, Maria, I can. I can speak to you. But I couldn't before when I tried. Do you know why?

Yes. I wasn't touching the magic.

I don't understand, he thought back.

I don't know if I do either. But if I want to mind-speak to you, I have to be in touch with the magic.

Are you?

Yes.

How?

I can't explain now. Lord Weedna will be here in a few hours, and we have to get away.

Then take two of their horses.

How?

Tristan slowly moved back to join her. He smiled as he shook his head. Maria thought she heard a silent laugh. She never imagined she would hear him laugh. *Ever since I met you, you have wanted one thing, to be a magician. Now you are. Magician, use your magic. Put them to sleep.*

Maria almost fell out of the tree when she released the branch and tried to cross her arms over her chest. Tristan steadied her. A month ago, there would have been anger in his eyes; now all he did was shake his head as he put her hands back on the branch and looked directly into her face. *Your way, Maria,* he thought. *Come.*

"Yes," she whispered, "my way." When they reached the ground, they listened. The four horses were farther away than before but still close enough to be heard. Jerold meowed and walked away. Maria and Tristan followed. When the sirnee stopped, so did they. Through the trees, Maria saw one of the soldiers.

She reached her mind out and when she felt the magic, whispered to it. *Make him sleep.* The soldier instantly drooped his head, dropped his sword, and fell off the horse. Tristan ran for the animal.

"There's one of them!" shouted a voice.

Maria turned. Three men, from three directions, were charging Tristan. "Sleep," she whispered three times as she looked at each man. But nothing happened. They continued to bear down on Tristan, who was holding the reins of the horse. He looked at her, eyes opened wide. The men were almost on top of him.

"It doesn't work!" she screamed as she stood up. "It doesn't work!"

"Aroo-eh! Aroo-eh!"

The soldiers saw her. Two of them turned their horses while the third continued straight.

Maria ran.

"Maagic! Use your maagic!" exploded a voice inside her head.

She remembered, but before she could concentrate, she tripped over a tree root. The horses pounded toward her. She held her breath — and tried to feel the magic. Tried to, but couldn't.

"Meow!"

Maria got up and ran.

"Get her!" shouted the rider, as he jumped off his animal.

"Where are you!" Maria shouted at the magic. The soldier lunged and managed to grab her ankle as he fell. Then he was on top of her, forcing her hands behind her back.

148

Maria's face was pushed into the ground as the soldier sat on her, trying to tie her hands.

Jerold attacked. He jumped, hitting the soldier's side, claws cutting deep into back and stomach. The man screamed and rolled off Maria, forcing Jerold to let go. "Aroo-eh."

Maria quickly rose. Tristan was struggling — he couldn't help her. The soldier she had fought had pulled a knife and was swinging it at Jerold — the sirnee couldn't help her either. *I have to do it alone. I have to believe in me.*

Maria closed her eyes — she thought to the magic. Her body tingled. *Sleep!*

The soldier fell. "Sleep," she whispered at the soldier who was still charging her on his horse. He did and somehow managed not to fall. The horse ran on past. "Sleep," she said to the third man who was wrestling Tristan. Maria started for Tristan but the forest swayed. Her legs wobbled. She put her hand on her head and clutched the nearest tree for support. Tristan was there holding her.

The magic stopped working when I told it to put the soldiers to sleep after the first man fell. I don't understand . . ."

But Tristan didn't wait. He quickly went back for two horses. After helping Maria mount, he got up, kicked the horse and raced away. Just before Maria started, she heard Jerold. The sirnee jumped onto Maria's saddle and she held him tightly.

They traveled back to the river, then south toward Kestra. For three hours, the horses walked or trotted or galloped along the river's bank. Maria didn't say anything.

She just thought about what had happened, trying to figure out why the magic hadn't listened to her. Maria rode silently. Finally, as the sun reached the top of the sky, Tristan stopped and they ate the few rations in the soldiers' saddle packs. Maria saw a pair of pants and a shirt that were only a little too big for her. She changed clothes; her dress was ready for the scrap heap. An hour after they stopped, they started again.

Tristan set a brisk pace. He knew that Lord Weedna would be coming after them. Maria soon grew tired. Her body hurt from bouncing in the saddle, but she didn't complain. Jerold didn't mind too much; at least that's what Maria thought. She had put him in the saddle pack. His head was out, front paws draped over the edge, the rest of his body inside. When the afternoon became evening, she wanted to tell Tristan to stop — wanted to but didn't. When he slowed, Jerold jumped out of the pack and headed for the nearest tree. All Maria wanted to do was sleep. Tristan woke her; a small fire burned just inside the treeline and two fish sizzled on a flat rock placed next to the coals. Jerold sat staring at them, tail straight up.

"Thanks for doing all this," she said as she stretched. By the time she had splashed some water on her face, the fish were done. Soon nothing but small bones licked clean were left. When Tristan lay down near the fire and slept, Maria did the same.

Later that night, when Pern had already circled his big brother several times, Maria woke up. Jerold was purring, rubbing his chin against her cheek. Her eyes opened.

"Rowl!"

Her first reaction was to roll over on her other side, but

when Jerold meowed a second time, she sat up. Ever since Jerold had found them, he had been telling her in a hundred different ways that sirnees were not just cats. They were something else, something Maria still didn't understand. If Jerold wanted her up, he had a good reason. She shook Tristan.

"Jerold woke me. Something's wrong."

Tristan was up quickly. The fire had burned out and the coals were cool to his touch, but he dropped the rock he had cooked the fish on over the ashes anyway. Then he got the horses, which were waiting nearby, saddled. Maria mounted, and they started.

But this time Jerold didn't jump onto the saddle. He ran ahead. In the cloudless sky, the twin moons gave the river and its bank an eerie glow and Jerold was easy to see. Peaceful night sounds filled the air, but the sirnee ignored them, never slowing, always moving. After almost an hour, Jerold stopped and turned east, away from the river.

Tristan held his horse as Maria started to follow Jerold. Maria looked back; he shook his head. He knew the geography of Yunii — she didn't. Something was in front of them, something Tristan wanted to avoid.

"We have to. Jerold knows what he's doing. He's always known. If I could talk to him, he'd probably tell me why he wants us to go that way. But I can't, so we just have to trust him."

Tristan was still hesitating when two sounds overpowered the calling crickets and male bullfrogs. The first was Jerold's meow; the second was an army trumpet. Tristan kicked his horse.

Jerold jumped on Maria's saddle and went into the

pack. He looked out, and whenever they veered away from where he wanted them to go, he meowed loudly.

The trumpets called. Though the sounds were far away, they never faded. *Weedna's seeking spell. Now that we're away from the water, it must be working.* As morning drew near and the sky lightened, the trees thinned — the sound of the pursuing soldiers continued to hound them.

The sun appeared over the horizon as the last trees fell behind. Jerold meowed and hopped down. Maria pulled on the reins. *No!* The sirnee had taken them to the one place in Yunii she knew about. The one place that no one ever went. Jerold had led them to The Dead Place, and the only way they could escape Lord Weedna was to enter it.

Chapter 15

Fairy tales were make-believe. Stories about elves, dwarfs, and goblins were fun to listen to and had entertained children for hundreds of years. But they were not true. Legends, on the other hand, were different. They, too, were stories; they, too, were probably make-believe. But somewhere in those stories was a touch of truth, a hint that, just maybe, the stories were real. The place that Maria and Tristan stood silently looking over was just such a hint.

Legend said that before the sorcerers disappeared, they fought among themselves. Why they fought or who won was not known. But the stories said they not only fought with men and horses, they also fought with magic — powerful magic. When children asked how their parents knew, the adults would always tell them of The Dead Place.

Tucked away between the southeast corner of Yunii and the northeast part of Kestra, was a large, almost perfectly half-moon-shaped piece of land, claimed by neither nation. The thickest part of that land ended when it touched the Thousand Mile Desert, and within its boundaries nothing lived. There was not one plant or tree, a single blade of grass, or a sole insect. Birds never flew over. Animals never entered. It was a place of death.

Maria had never seen The Dead Place, but she knew it at once from its description. Everything on the land was black; an ancient fire had scorched the land, burning everything within. Then a sorcerer's magic had sealed it. The charred tree trunks stood tall — leafless and twigless. The black charcoal ash from leaves, branches, and grass still covered the land, frozen, ice hard. Maria searched the horizon, but the only thing she saw was blackness.

Jerold meowed and started. As soon as his foot touched the edge of The Dead Place, he meowed again, louder. But he didn't turn around; he didn't stop.

Tristan dismounted and waited for Maria. He shook his head, let out a deep breath, and began walking. But the horse wouldn't go. It reared up, neighing loudly, and violently pulled its head back. It wouldn't step onto the black earth.

Maria didn't try to lead her horse. She took the saddle pack off, draped it over her shoulders, and waited for Tristan to do the same. Then they followed Jerold.

When Maria's feet touched the solid ash, her whole body shuddered. A feeling of overwhelming sadness flowed through her. Instantly, she recalled the moment Eonoway had told her that her parents had died. She remembered how she had felt. A pain swelled in her chest. The emptiness in her stomach returned, and with it the feeling of being hopelessly lost, alone, without an anchor to hold her on Enstor. She cried and tears dripped, unwiped, down her cheek.

She heard a sound — her head turned. Tristan, walking

next to her, was crying. As the tears ran down his face, he had sobbed. He did it only once, but it was a long, deep cry. Though his tears kept coming, they now came in silence. Maria wondered what he was reliving.

A single clap of thunder exploded over them. It was so loud that she bent low and covered her head, but when she looked up, the sky was clear. The sun beat down on them.

"Meeeooww!" The sirnee's call reminded Maria of when they had all stood looking at huge trees growing on the other side of a river.

Tristan squeezed her hand as they walked farther into the land. The stabbing sadness had left, but its presence hovered over them. Traveling was difficult; the ground was so hard that knife-sharp edges cut into the soles of their shoes. Maria winced the first time she felt pain and they slowed, searching the ground before taking a step. Tristan moved in front, pointing to the back of his feet, telling her to step where he did.

"Mew. Mew." Maria saw tiny drops of red on the black earth. The sirnee had cut his paws but continued walking. Their journey through The Dead Place was slow. Several times Jerold stopped and forced Tristan and Maria to back up as he looked for an easier way. The third time the sirnee halted, Maria saw a small trail of blood Jerold was leaving behind. Twice she had cried out when the sharp earth cut through her shoes, but most of the time her soles were thick enough to protect her feet. Jerold, however, had no protection; his paws were bloody. Worried, she picked him up.

"Let me carry you. You can't walk here."

But Jerold began to twist and turn. He meowed and

would have jumped down if Maria hadn't gently placed him on a patch of smooth earth.

Trumpets sounded behind them. Someone had found their horses and was calling Lord Weedna and the rest of the soldiers.

"At least we don't have to worry about them. They won't be able to travel any faster than we can."

Tristan looked at the sky. Then he touched his chest, her chest, and pointed to his right. Next, he pointed to Jerold, and then straight ahead, the direction Jerold was leading them.

"I don't understand," she said. "Wait a minute! I forgot about the magic. I'll try to touch it, then we can mind-speak." Maria closed her eyes and let her mind drift.

"Meow! Meow!"

A cold darkness swamped her. She gasped. Her body shivered violently; her mind plunged into a frozen well — thick, rich, oozing evil seized her. She screamed.

Maria felt a stinging across her face; her mind came back and her eyes opened. Tristan was there, shaking her shoulders. She took a breath and leaned into him. His arms circled her tightly.

"Rowl."

"I touched something . . . something evil. I can't use the magic here. Don't you do it, either. Come on, the faster we leave, the better I'll like it."

But again Tristan pointed. This time, he pointed first to the sun, and then made an east-west arch with his arm.

"I think I understand," she said. "Kestra is south of us but Jerold is heading east, toward the desert."

156

Tristan nodded.

"I don't know why he's going this way, but look at him. Though he's bleeding and hurt, he's not stopping. He's going in the direction he wants us to go. We're going to follow him."

When evening came, they were completely surrounded by The Dead Place. Jerold had veered slightly, but continued heading more east than south. On a patch of smooth earth, Jerold stopped. When he sat and began licking his paws, Maria knew it was time to camp. She sat, too, and picked him up. He started to squiggle but she held him tightly under his shoulders while his body dangled in the air.

"Now you listen to me!" she said into his face. "Every time you've told us what to do we've listened. When you walked into this place we followed. When Tristan said we weren't going in the right direction, we still followed. Now it's your turn to listen. Your paws are cut and licking will only open the cuts more. You're going to sit down and let me wash and wrap them. Understand!"

Jerold looked at her and licked the end of her nose. He stopped squirming.

Maria put him in her lap and took the water bag from her pack. She wet a cloth and wiped each of Jerold's paws clean. Then she tore it into several strips and wrapped one around each paw. When she put Jerold down, he stayed. Dinner was a ration of water and then the three of them slept.

Maria dreamed. Men — tall, handsome, and pointed-eared riding huge white horses — looked afraid as an army ran after them. Blood appeared on their hands, swords dropped to the ground. She saw a river with huge trees on its far bank. The fleeing men crossed the river and disappeared, and finally all she saw were trees. When she woke, her eyes were red, the ground damp where she had wept, and though she couldn't remember the dream — couldn't remember why she had cried — she felt a loss, a great and terrible loss.

Jerold meowed in the predawn darkness. It was time to leave. He again refused to let Maria carry him, but he didn't disturb the cloth tied around his paws. After an hour, the fabric was soaked red. Though he walked slower, Jerold stubbornly kept moving forward.

A trumpet. As the sun rose, Maria turned and saw far in the distance the shapes of men coming after them.

"How could they move that fast?"

Tristran pointed to his shoes and touched his calf.

"They have boots."

He nodded.

"Jerold," she said, as she sped up to reach him. "We have to go faster. I'm going to carry you whether you like it or not." Jerold didn't like it, but he was smart enough not to argue.

Maria and Tristan walked faster. The sharp ground cut into them; they couldn't take the time to plan where they would step — they just walked. Maria pressed her teeth together as the glass-hard ground cut into the bottom of her feet. She held Tristan's hand and each time she felt the razor edge cutting her, she squeezed. He didn't mind.

Soon her feet felt as if they were on fire. Tristan had to

feel the same; he limped every time he put his right foot down. The men following were still there, far in the distance. Maria and Tristan were matching their pace.

Jerold meowed. He was sitting in the saddle pack watching the land. Maria turned. He meowed a second time when she faced south. They changed directions. When the three stopped briefly to rest, Jerold hungrily lapped up the water Maria spilled into her palm. She and Tristan drank their rations, too. They continued.

The sun moved high; its heat burned them. The emptiness in Maria's stomach gnawed; they had no food when they entered The Dead Place and would find none until they left it. Their water was almost gone, too. Maria searched the horizon but saw only blackness. She let out a breath and kept moving, holding Tristan's hand as tightly as he held hers. She wanted to talk but had no energy.

They walked the rest of the day and by the time they stopped, both were limping badly. Maria drank deeply, and together with Tristan and Jerold finished the last of their water. "It's gone. Until we leave, we have nothing else."

As they stretched out on the flattest ground they could find, Maria's feet pounded inside her shoes. When she began to untie the laces, Tristan stopped her. "All right," she whispered, as she lay down on the hard earth. "I'll leave them on." She never knew if Tristan heard her answer; her head went down and she was asleep. This night, she slept without dreaming, and when Jerold woke them, it was early dawn.

Tristan was up and reached down to help her stand.

When she put her weight on her feet, she jumped at him and pressed her face into his chest. It was the only way she could muffle her scream. Blood dripped down her chin from where she had bitten her lip. She held on to Tristan, pressing her hands into his shoulders. The pain eased.

"Mew."

Tears came from the corners of her eyes; gingerly she took a step. It hurt, but she took another and another. Tristan stopped her. He looked deep into her eyes, and placed both of his hands on her cheeks. He smiled — she giggled. He looked like the Tristan Lin had yelled at long ago, dirty face, torn clothes. He leaned forward and kissed her gently. Then he took her hand and started walking.

In the hazy sky, Maria could not see the men who followed. Boots or not, they also must have been exhausted, and they did not have a sirnee to wake them so early.

Jerold led and would not let Maria pick him up. He set an easy pace and after several hours of slow progress, suddenly turned and headed due west. The pain was constant now, but it didn't stop Maria from lifting her feet up and putting them down.

Tristan saw it first and pointed. Far ahead of them — green on the horizon. He walked faster. Maria leaned on him as she hobbled forward. Jerold meowed. He, too, went faster.

Maria's head was down. She watched the ground and tried to avoid the sharp peaks that were everywhere. Each time they stopped for a moment, she looked up. The green was still far away. "Why isn't it closer? We've been walking for an hour. We must be near the end. Why isn't it here?"

Tristan didn't answer. He put his arm around her waist

and started again. Maria kept even with him. Eventually the horizon came to them. She could see trees and grass. She moved faster. Together with Tristan and Jerold, they ran the last few hundred yards. When they finally reached it, when they finally stepped on real ground and felt it give way just a little under their weight, all Maria wanted to do was fall. But Tristan wouldn't let her. He pointed back to The Dead Place. Somewhere behind them, Lord Weedna was coming for them. Tristan held her arm, half leading, half pulling her into the forest.

"Are we still in Yunii?" she managed to say.

Tristan shrugged his shoulders. The river started at the Azure Lake in northern Yunii, went south though Kestra and eventually became the natural border between Ekloy and Mikloner. The forest that Jerold had led them out of when they first entered The Dead Place also bridged Yunii and Kestra. There was no way of knowing. But where they were wouldn't matter if the men following caught them. So two humans and one sirnee forced themselves to walk through the trees, forced themselves to continue heading westward toward the river. It took several hours but they found it. It looked just the same as the first time — wide, slow-moving, crystal clear.

Maria plunged into it, clothes and all. She drank it, rubbed it over her head, and drank it some more. She sat on the bank, took off her shoes, and threw them away. There was practically nothing left of their soles. Her feet swelled. The water caused sparks of pain to shoot through them, but Maria welcomed it. It was a good pain, a cleansing pain.

A few minutes later, she heard a muffled meow. Turning, she saw Jerold sitting near her with a squirrel. He dropped it and disappeared again into the woods. Tristan limped over to the dead animal and began preparing it for the fire. He motioned to Maria, who crawled over to him, picking up small branches along the way. Soon, the fire was going and the squirrel cooking. Jerold returned. This time, he had a bird.

The three ate. Twice more, Jerold left their camp, and twice more returned with something to eat. As the sun sank low so the light of the twin moons could shine, Maria and Tristan slept. Their clothes were still damp but their stomachs were full. Jerold slept with them, curled up in a ball leaning against Maria's side. The sirnee was tired, so tired that he didn't hear a small party of men approaching just before the twin moons disappeared.

Chapter 16

Maria was not awakened by a gentle nudge from Jerold. Someone rolled her over and before she realized she wasn't dreaming, her hands were securely tied behind her back. She was roughly pulled to her feet and dragged over to the nearest tree. The soldier forced her down and tied her to it. Tristan was tied to one next to her. Jerold had vanished into the forest.

The men didn't talk. They went to the water and pulled their boots off. They grunted and ahhed as the water cooled their feet. When they had had enough, they carefully put their boots back on.

"Magician–lord or not," said one of the men, "that's the last time I'm ever going into The Dead Place."

"Tell that to Lord Weedna when he gets here. Armand, take that crossbow of yours and catch something to cook." As the soldier slowly walked into the woods, the others collected wood and started a fire. They sat silently, breathing heavily.

Maria was just waking. Her feet had stung when the soldier first pulled her up, but the pain was easing now. The morning fog cleared from her head and she looked at Tristan, who was staring at her.

She tried to relax as she closed her eyes and felt the trunk of the tree roughly scraping against her head. This time, when she called to the magic, it heard. Her mind left and when it entered the earth, she felt the magic flow into her. *Tristan, can you hear me?*

Yes. I'm glad we're out of The Dead Place. It's good to talk again.

Shall I put them to sleep while I'm connected to the magic?

No. They're waiting for the Yuniian magician. Let's wait for him, too. If his power is weak near water, you should be able to fight him with your magic. Maybe he knows about the army that left for Kestra.

But what if he's too powerful? I'm just learning.

Listen to me, Maria Ronlin. You ARE a magician! You must believe that. We mind-speak and no one has done that in hundreds of years. I didn't discover it; you did. Tristan smiled at her. *You must believe in yourself.* Maria nodded. *Good.* He paused for a moment before continuing. *Tell me — how do you do it? How can we mind-speak? How do you touch the magic?*

But you do it all the time. You make fire . . . you healed my arm. You talk to it, don't you?

I think to the magic and ask it things. Sometimes it listens, sometimes it doesn't. I couldn't find a way to make it listen all the time. Neither could Lin or Befany — neither can you. That's the nature of magic and you must accept it. Now tell me what you do.

164

Do you remember when I broke the spell Lord Tajor had put on us? I told you that my mind left my body. Tristan, it wasn't my imagination. It really happened. If I concentrate, I can force my mind out of my body and into the elements. The earth is the strongest. That's where I feel the magic most. But magic is all around us. I've felt it in the air, in the water, and in the fire. Close your eyes. Let your mind float. Try it. I used a tree to help me. I made my mind enter the wood and follow the trunk into the earth. Think of the tree behind you. See it with your mind. Enter it, follow the trunk down, find the magic.

Tristan leaned back. After a moment, his body shivered — chills also raced along Maria's shoulders. She knew before his words entered her mind that he had found the magic.

It IS there. I felt it! Do you know what this means? As long as one of us is connected to the magic we can mindspeak. If I can't reach the magic next time I try, but you do, we can talk to each other. And if you can't reach it, then maybe I can.

Do you think everyone will be able to find the magic? she thought.

He smiled. *No. Magic doesn't listen to everyone. We know that. It also doesn't listen all the time. We know that, too. Magic listens to whom it wants, when it wants. We have to keep this a secret, you and I. Befany must know so we can free Lin. But no one else, not until we find out more about the power this new way of using magic will bring.*

A noise caused them to look up. A tired-looking Lord of Yunii, with a torn and ripped cloak, appeared out of the

165

forest. Before heading to water, however, he stood before Maria and Tristan.

"When I come back, you will tell me what I wish to know. Then, as payment for the chase you led me on, one of you will die. The other will live just long enough to speak of Jerbin's treachery to the king."

The soldier who had left with the crossbow returned carrying a baby deer over his shoulders. Tristan stared at him. No one noticed that after the man put the deer near the fire, he sat down and fell over.

When the magician comes back, thought Tristan, *freeze him in his position.*

Maria's answer was cut off by the shadow of Lord Weedna. "I've decided which of you will die." Her eyes opened wide. She looked at Tristan, who only smiled back.

Believe, Maria.

Maria looked at the red-robed lord. He had a knife in his hand; a smile on his face. But he didn't move. The soldiers behind him collapsed. The ropes binding Maria and Tristan fell.

I told you, Maria. If you believe you can do something, then most of the time you can. And if you can't, it's not you, it's the way of the magic. Tristan got up and helped Maria. The bottoms of her feet were sore and she hobbled to the magician who was staring at her.

"Where is the army going to enter Kestra?"

Lord Weedna's mouth opened. Maria saw him struggle, trying not to answer. "They . . . will enter . . . from the Plain of Sroomooth."

"Why there? That's the main border between the two

countries. Surely Queen Andraya will know they are coming and bring her army to meet yours."

Again, Lord Weedna struggled not to answer. But he was too weak to fight Maria's magic.

"It is a trap. The two other . . . armies . . . in Kestra now . . . are chasing Andraya. They are both on the Plain of Sroomooth. Andraya is somewhere between them. The plan is to trap . . . to trap Queen Andraya's army. The two armies . . . will force Andraya to flee . . . north . . . "

"Go on," said Maria.

"Northward. As she does, they will come together. The combined force will . . . will attack just before the new army reaches Andraya. While the . . . while the . . . Kestran army is fighting the combined Yuniian army, they will be attacked from the rear. Kestra will be defeated."

"I order you to go home and stay there. You are not to tell anyone about this. Never. Do you understand?" When he didn't answer, she closed her eyes and felt the magic. Then she said it again.

"Yes," he answered.

"Good. Now get out of here. Pick up your soldiers, and leave." Maria broke away from the magic. She felt tired and was glad Tristan was there so she could lean on him. Lord Weedna balled his hands into tight fists. Then he turned, walked stiffly to his men, and shook them awake. They grunted to themselves, but followed the lord when he started walking.

"I did it! I made the magic obey me."

Tristan, who had started cutting up the deer, looked at her as he threw raw scraps to Jerold.

167

"We have to leave," Maria said. "We have to find the queen. We have to warn her."

She saw Tristan close his eyes. *One day won't matter. We'll stay here and rest. The deer will give us enough meat so we won't go hungry and its hide will fix our shoes. Speaking of shoes, yours are over there. Get them. When I cure the hide a bit, I'll fix both of ours.*

Maria couldn't argue because what he said made sense. When they started, she still limped, but her pack was full, her feet well padded.

The next day, they swam the river and reached the western side. Jerold, the last to jump into the water, meowed most of the way just to tell Maria and Tristan he didn't like it.

"You know," she said to the sirnee as he shook himself dry, "you never complained when you walked over the dead land and cut your paws. How come you complain so loudly when you get a little wet?"

Jerold looked at her but didn't answer. He just sat and licked himself.

Tristan headed southwest. The Plain of Sroomooth stretched west of the forest once the river crossed into Kestra, and that's where they had to go. It took them three days to reach it. The first day they made camp early — their feet were too sore for a long march. But by the time they stood overlooking the plain, they could spend the day walking, though not as fast as either would have liked. Now, for at least a hundred miles west of them and maybe eighty or ninety south, the land was rich and fertile. They traveled quickly, hoping to find a town or a village. They had to get some horses or else their warning would come too late. On the evening of the second day, they saw a sign: "Preenlate, one mile." It was a small town, similar to Ventor, and when they reached it, there was only one inn where they could go.

But the inn was crowded. Maria and Tristan had to push their way though the people in order to see what was happening. At the far end of the common room, the innkeeper had set up a long table. Sitting behind it were two lesser magicians, each wearing a brown robe of office.

"What's going on?" asked Maria.

The man turned and looked at them. He took Maria and Tristan to the side. "The Queen's Voices are collecting taxes," he whispered. "They are using their truth spells to find out what we have, and are asking for all of it. They have the tax rolls, and if a person does not answer to his name, they will confiscate everything his family has. We have to be here. But you don't. Get out before they see you."

"But that's not fair," said Maria. "Queen Andraya would never order such a thing."

"That's what we said, but they told us the war is not going well and the queen needs to hire mercenaries from Ekloy or Mikloner."

"But the truth spell," she said. "They cannot use it for such a thing as this. The Order of Magicians would never allow it."

"But they are of the Order," said the man.

Tristan touched her — she heard his voice. *There is no law that says all magicians must be good. We know that from Yunii. We know that from The Dead Place.*

How dare they! Maria pushed her way toward the table

169

where the lesser magicians sat. This time, Tristan followed her. Before the magician holding the scroll could read the next name, Maria called out.

"By whose authority do you use the truth spell to collect this money?"

The men looked up. They made faces when they saw who spoke. Maria looked like a street beggar: tangled hair, dirty face and hands, wearing wrinkled men's clothing that was too big for her.

"Throw this baggage in the street," said the one reading the names.

But as a man stepped to her, Maria raised her voice. "I am Maria Ronlin, former apprentice to Eonoway, Magician of the First Order. I accuse you of using the magic illegally. I accuse you of turning the true magic dark. The Order of Magicians would never agree to this, and it is my right as a Kestran citizen to ask the names of those who gave you your orders!"

"Aroo-eh." Jerold was somewhere on the floor of the crowded room.

The man with the scroll rose. "I have ordered her thrown out. Now I order her killed for insulting the Order of Magicians." He was tall and stared down at Maria.

Maria heard something familiar in his voice. The tone he used was the same the Yuniian Lords used when they spoke to their people. *That man IS evil, and could wear a red robe just as easily as he does the brown. Tristan was right. The lost magic must be kept a secret, even from the Order of Magicians.*

She reached out with her mind and sought the magic. But there was no tingle, no power. Someone grabbed her; Tristan shoved the man aside, then turned Maria around and looked into her eyes. He touched her cheek; she smiled and sent her mind out. It found the power — she knew it would listen to her. "Stop! By the Order of Magicians, I order you to stand before me!" The man sitting shot to his feet. The one standing straightened his back. The two stood like statues before Maria. The people pushed back, giving her room. Maria heard only silence.

"Who told you to collect this money?"

"No . . . one," they answered together.

"What do you plan to do with it?"

"Keep it . . . for . . . ourselves,"

"Remove your robes. I forbid you to practice magic again. I order you to go to the capital and present yourself to the Order of Magicians. I order you to confess your crimes, and tell them that you used the truth spell to steal from the people of Preenlate. Do you understand? You are to tell them you used the truth spell to steal money from our people!"

"Yes," they answered, dropping their robes. The villagers parted for them as they headed for the door.

"Who is the record keeper of this town?" Maria asked.

"I am," answered a voice.

"Can you return what those two took?"

"Yes, Magician."

"Then do so." Maria became tired and leaned on the table.

You did it, Maria.

"Yes, Magician," answered the record keeper. "Thank you. We all thank you."

"Where is the innkeeper?"

171

"Here, Magician."

"We have no money. Will you give us a floor to sleep on? We carry an urgent message for the queen and ask you to find someone to lend us two horses."

"You will have my best room, Magician. And a meal, two horses, and since you seek the queen, we will give you both clothes to wear. You cannot see Andraya dressed like that."

"But I told you, we can't pay for any of those things."

"You paid for it with your service. The people of Preenlate will always remember you, Maria Ronlin. And when we speak of this night, we will also remember with pride how we helped you in return."

"Thank you," answered Maria. "Then can I ask for one more favor?" When the innkeeper nodded, she whispered to him. "Can we have two hot baths?" He laughed as he put one hand on her shoulder and the other on Tristan's. Tristan did not back away.

In the morning when they left Preenlate, Maria wore a new brown dress. Tristan wore a new shirt and pants also. The horses they rode were old, but they trotted steadily deeper into the Plain of Sroomooth. Jerold rode in Maria's saddle pack, looking out over the miles and miles of fields and tall wavy grass. For the rest of that day, and the following two, they saw nothing. It was not until the morning of the fourth that something appeared on the horizon.

As they continued riding southwest, cutting across the plain, they saw smoke in the distance. Hundreds of tiny spirals drifted into the clear sky. Maria concentrated. This time, the magic quickly entered her. *I think we've found them,* she thought.

But who? Tristan thought back. *Queen Andraya's men or Helborat's?*

Maria shook her head as they continued. Half an hour later, their question was answered. Riders appeared, facing the two of them.

Can you see who they are?

Tristan leaned up in the saddle and stared. *I don't see a purple banner. They must be Yuniian soldiers.*

I can put them to sleep.

That's only a patrol. You can't put an army to sleep.

I don't want to kill, Tristan. We just discovered how to talk to the magic and we have no idea what it can really do. I don't want to tell it to kill. We saw what can happen if magic is used for evil when we were in The Dead Place.

Yunii attacked us, remember?

Their king ordered it. Most of Helborat's soldiers are just like ours. They're men doing what they were told. If Andraya ordered her army to attack Ekloy, the soldiers would do it. They'd have to. If we've really found the ancient magic Lord Weedna spoke about, I don't want it to wake after a thousand years just to have it destroy. There must be a better way. We have to find it, Tristan.

Let's hope we have time, he thought back as the two turned their horses and raced away from the approaching soldiers.

Chapter 17

"Rowl. Rowl!" When Maria kept urging her horse on, Jerold squirmed out of the saddle pack and jumped down.

"He doesn't want us to go."

The soldiers were closer now. Maria could see the dirt on their faces as they bore down. She closed her eyes and searched for the magic. But before she could find it, the horses slowed. One by one, the riders slipped out of the saddle.

"Did you . . ."

They're just sleeping. I understand why you get tired after using the magic. It was easy putting a few men to sleep. But the more power you use, the more energy it takes. We have to be careful as we learn how to use the magic.

"We?"

Tristan smiled.

"We may not have time. Jerold stopped us for a reason. What if we have reached the outer line of the Yuniian army? What if this isn't the new army, but one that has been in Kestra all summer? What if Queen Andraya is already trapped?"

That's a lot of if's, isn't it?

Jerold meowed again.

Maria felt a hole open in her stomach. Hearing Jerold told her what she had guessed was true.

What do you want to do?

"We have to get to the queen. We have to help."

How? We don't have enough power to put two armies to sleep, and I don't know how to defeat an army without killing.

Maria couldn't answer. She and Tristan watched while the soldiers slept and their horses grazed. It was so peaceful Maria found it hard to believe that a battle could be taking place just over the horizon. "We have to go."

Tristan didn't answer. He shrugged his shoulders and shook his head. But he followed when she headed in the direction the Yuniian soldiers had come from.

Soon they saw smoke, then tent tops appeared. They were approaching from the rear and there were no more guards.

What do you want to do? thought Tristan.

"I don't know," she answered as they entered the camp.

Just then, trumpets sounded. Soldiers ran from their tents fully dressed for war: stiff leather vests, high boots, shields of leather stretched over wooden frames, and swords strapped to their sides. Many had bows or crossbows with quivers filled with arrows. In the uproar, no one paid any attention to two extra riders.

Maria and Tristan moved with the flow of men who ran through the camp to large rope fences where hundreds of horses were tied. Somehow, even in the confusion and the noise, soldiers found their own horses and mounted up. They formed small companies; the companies linked together to make battalions. When the battalions moved out, Maria and Tristan went with them.

Once they left the camp, the army began a slow trot northwest and rode close to half an hour before stopping. They then spread out, forming long lines, twelve deep. Officers shouted orders and the first two lines rode several hundred yards forward before stopping. Another set of orders and the next two lines rode a hundred yards before they stopped. Soon, the Yuniian army was in six groups, each one two lines thick. Maria and Tristan, sandwiched in the second line of the first group, saw what they faced.

Ahead was the Kestran army, men in shiny leather vests and polished swords. In front of them were riders wearing purple robes. *Magicians of the First Order. I wonder if Eonoway is there.* She remembered the overconfident captain who had collected Lin's tax. He said Kestran soldiers were better trained than Yuniian ones and he was right. Kestra was the smallest of the four nations and one of the other three countries always wanted to get bigger. But being better trained might not help on this day. She looked down the rows of men she and Tristan sat next to, then turned and looked behind. Queen Andraya's army was outnumbered five or six to one. Maria settled back in her saddle. She didn't need Jerold's sixth sense to tell her that the new army, the one from the north, was somewhere behind the queen. If that army was half the size of the Yuniian men who now faced the queen, Kestra would not survive this battle.

A trumpet sounded, and from the far side of the Yuniian lines, magician-lords appeared. Maria counted more than twenty as they walked their horses toward the center of their soldiers' lines. Then they marched forward, stopping only a hundred yards before the Magicians of the First Order. One of magician-lords spoke, and his voice carried to every ear on the battlefield.

"Men of Kestra, throw down your arms. Swear allegiance to King Helborat, and all, except your queen, shall live. Kestra is no more. You are all citizens of Yunii. Give fealty to your new king."

From the first line of Kestran soldiers, waves of arrows took flight. But halfway between the Yuniian magicians and the Kestran line, the arrows slammed into an invisible wall and bounced harmlessly to the ground.

Jerold, who rode in the saddle pack, burred softly. Maria's horse moved, and though the men on both sides of her called, no one stopped her or Tristan as the two entered the space between the armies.

They guided their horses around the line of magician-lords. The one speaking was still calling to the queen's soldiers to surrender, and none of the red-robed men paid any attention as the two walked closer to Andraya's line. But when they turned and cut in front of them, the lord stopped speaking. Magicians in both red and purple stared in disbelief at the young riders standing alone between the two armies.

I'm going to break the wall.

You understand what will happen? answered Tristan. *If the wall fails, some of the lords will die.*

"I know. But I have to, don't I?"

"Aroo-eh."

Yes, thought Tristan, *you do.*

Please, be there! Maria reached for the magic and felt the tingles. Then she turned and looked to the Kestran soldiers. "Fire your arrows again."

A purple-robed man raised and lowered his arm, as a second host of arrows took flight. Maria spoke to her magic. "Break their wall."

Four of the Yuniian magicians fell as arrows pierced their robes. The rest pulled on the reins and their horses backed up.

"Who are you to defy us?" shouted one of the magician-lords.

"You have no right here. Your magic is dark. It's evil and has no place in this land."

"Our magic will rule here. Your queen sends children to fight her battles, and children should know their place!"

"Your magic is dying. Your scrolls have burned. You have nothing to teach your apprentices; you have nothing to remind you of what you have forgotten."

"We will copy the scrolls in Bolstane when we take the capital. Send your arrows again, men of Kestra. See what happens when children do men's work."

A third flight of arrows rose up. Maria spoke to her magic, but the arrows fell before reaching their goal.

"You cannot defeat us, soldiers of Kestra," called a Yuniian magician. "You are outnumbered by those who face you, and even as we speak, another army comes at you from behind. Give way to us and live. Stand against us and die." In one motion, the Yuniian magicians turned their horses and rode back. In a minute, Maria, Tristan, and Jerold were all that separated the two armies.

Maria was silent. *What should I do,* she thought.

An unknown but familiar voice entered her head. *Maagic. Maagic.*

Maria looked at Tristan, who was smiling at her. He reached out and took her hand. *Use your magic, love,* he thought.

"How?" she whispered.

He shrugged his shoulders. *Let your imagination go. Lin always said that that was the key to performing magic. Do whatever you want to. The magic will be there. I will be there.*

Maria closed her eyes and grabbed his hand. Her mind left, seeking strength from the four elements. It divided; part went down and felt the cool earth. Part reached out to the heat of the hundreds of fires that burned in the Kestran army camp. And part soared up into the clouds, into the wind.

Her eyes opened when the first trumpets of the attack sounded.

"Aroo-eh. Aroo-eh."

"No!" she shouted, and her voice drowned out the battle cries as if they were whispers. "By the ancient four, I order you to stop. There shall be no war!"

Power, more power than Maria imagined possible, poured into her. She clasped Tristan's hand as strong winds began blowing into the Yuniian army. From the white clouds above, lightning flashed down, frightening horses and making them throw their riders. Solid streams of water gushed out of holes that suddenly opened in the clouds and drenched the Yuniian magicians.

Maria felt weak. The magic was draining her. Tristan

saw her sway in the saddle and jumped down to help her off. His voice entered her mind. *Stop, rest. I will follow your lead.* Maria breathed deeply as she released the magic. But the wind continued; the lightning flashed; the water still poured.

Maria looked at the havoc they had created. She heard Yuniian officers screaming at their men, urging them forward. She saw the soldiers begin to regroup and knew their magic wasn't enough. Now it was Tristan who weaved.

"It's no good! We have to do something else."

Tristan let go of the air and the wind stopped. He let go of the fire and the lightning stopped. He let go of the water and the rain stopped.

Jerold stood on the ground between them. *Earrth. Seeek the earrth. Deeeper. Deeeper.*

Maria closed her eyes and concentrated. Her mind plunged. When she thought she would fall, when she was sure that her mind could go no farther, the voice returned.

Deeeper. And with the voice came a spurt of strength. A new and alien energy entered her.

"Aroo-eh!"

Maria struggled to stand straight. She felt Tristan's hand and had the oddest feeling that his mind had joined hers, had become one with hers. Renewed, her mind, coupled with Tristan's and something she didn't understand, moved forward.

Down it went until it reached the water table. Maria felt cleansed — pure — refreshed by water filtered through tons of earth and rocks. The fatigue left.

Deeeper.

Maria willed her mind farther. Just beneath the water,

flowing under it inside the solid rock, her mind entered the ancient magic. Magic that had been trapped for a thousand years flooded into her like torrents of a raging river. Tristan's hand squeezed tighter. Jerold meowed. Maria stood tall and opened her eyes. She was Maria — she was the four. She was the earth and the air. She was the fire and the water. She *was* the magic.

The wind blew, throwing the leading soldiers back. The lightning struck, hitting the red magicians, killing them and the magic they were trying to wield. The rain came, soaking everyone who wore Yuniian colors. Maria thought to the earth and it answered. A low rumbling sound overpowered the trumpets. The grass swayed — the earth trembled. Horses slipped and fell. Men dropped their swords and held on to each other to keep from falling. The earthquake spread from Maria outward, but the Kestran soldiers who watched, frozen, unbelieving, felt nothing. When the ground stopped shaking, not one Yuniian soldier was on his feet, and after the last tremor faded, not one Yuniian soldier dared to rise.

Orders were shouted behind Maria and the Kestran army surged forward. They ran to the fallen soldiers, taking swords and knives, bows and arrows, but not lives. Maria looked into Tristan's face and his black eyes smiled at her.

"Did you call me love?" she whispered. She fainted before he could answer.

Maria had never been so tired. She stretched and felt a blanket. She moved and felt a mattress.

"Maria," a voice called. "Can you hear me?"

181

Maria knew that voice. Eonoway, her teacher. *Oh no, I've overslept! I'll be late for my lessons!* Instantly, her eyes opened and she sat up.

"It's all right," said Eonoway. "You're safe. We're all safe. When the new army from Yunii heard what happened, they turned and ran. The rest of the Yuniian soldiers will have a long walk home. You did it, Maria. I wish I could say it was my teaching that made you so powerful, but I would fool myself if I did."

"Mistress," whispered Maria.

"No, Maria. I am not your mistress any longer. You are my equal. You are more than my equal. You called on powers that have slept for ages and they answered you."

Maria yawned and quickly covered her mouth with her hand.

"Sleep, child," said Eonoway. "You are a Magician of the First Order, just as you have always wanted. Later you can tell us what you did and how you did it. We have time, child, lots of time." With that, Eonoway got up and left the tent.

"Aroo-eh." Jerold jumped on the bed and purred as he rubbed the side of his chin against Maria's.

"Hi," said Maria, yawning again. Then she looked up. The tent was empty. *Tristan!* She concentrated and thought of the magic. It was hard. Her head hurt and it took her a moment to feel the tingle. *Tristan. Tristan! Where are you?*

I'm in the camp. I have enough supplies to reach Deventap without stopping.

When are you going?

As soon as I fill my water bag.

What do you mean 'As soon as I fill MY water bag'? I hope you're filling mine, too.

But Eonoway has declared you a Magician of the First Order. Isn't that what you always wanted?

I wanted to be a magician, Tristan. And I am. I have my own shoes now, and I don't want anyone to tell me to wear different ones. I have everything I want and I don't need the Order of Magicians to give me anything else. Besides, there are two things I have to do. First, I have to help you free Lin.

And the second?

I have to hear your answer about what you called me.

There was no mistaking Tristan's answer. He *was* laughing. *We'll talk on the way. I can see the tent you're in. You can't leave through the front. There are too many people. Slip out under the back and I'll meet you. With all the riders coming and going, no one will notice us leaving.*

And when the three of them left, no one did.